Date Due

OCT 0 9 2006			
MAY 0 3 2001			

D0961722

FIC
SOU

Southgate, Martha.

Another way to
dance

24123

Another Way to Dance

F₁c
sou

MARTHA SOUTHGATE

LAUREL-LEAF BOOKS

LELAND HIGH SCHOOL

Published by
Bantam Doubleday Dell Books for Young Readers
a division of
Bantam Doubleday Dell Publishing Group, Inc.
1540 Broadway
New York, New York 10036

If you purchased this book without a cover you should be aware that this book is stolen property. It was reported as "unsold and destroyed" to the publisher and neither the author nor the publisher has received any payment for this "stripped book."

Special thanks to the New Jersey Ballet.

Copyright © 1996 by Martha Southgate
Cover illustration by Todd L. W. Doney

All rights reserved. No part of this book may be reproduced or transmitted in any form or by any means, electronic or mechanical, including photocopying, recording, or by any information storage and retrieval system, without the written permission of the Publisher, except where permitted by law. For information address Delacorte Press, 1540 Broadway, New York, New York 10036.

The trademark Laurel-Leaf Library® is registered in the U.S. Patent and Trademark Office.
The trademark Dell® is registered in the U.S. Patent and Trademark Office.

Visit us on the Web! www.bdd.com

Educators and librarians, visit the BDD Teacher's Resource Center at www.bdd.com/teachers

ISBN: 0-440-21968-X

RL: 5.3

Reprinted by arrangement with Delacorte Press
Printed in the United States of America
February 1998
OPM 10 9 8 7 6 5 4 3

This book is dedicated to my son, Nathaniel G.S. Phillips, who is already a great joy and a great dancer, and to my husband, Jeff Phillips, who shares the challenge of making our life together with a joyous spirit and a loving heart.

There are girls who do not like real life. When they hear the harsh belches of its engines approaching along the straight road that leads from childhood, through adolescence, to adultery, they dart into a side turning. When they take their hands away from their eyes, they find themselves in the gallery of the ballet. There they sit for many years feeding their imaginations on those fitful glimpses of a dancer's hand or foot. When I was young I too "adored" the ballet. For me its charm was that one of the dancers might break his neck, but what appeals to these girls is the moonlit atmosphere of love and death.

—Quentin Crisp, *The Naked Civil Servant*

Acknowledgments

I owe a great debt of thanks to the following:

The Master of Fine Arts in Writing program at Goddard College, particularly my advisors, Jacqueline Woodson, Andrea Freud Loewenstein, and Jan Clausen. They held open the door and pushed me to walk through it. This book might not exist without them.

Lareese Hall, for two years of being a great writing-school roomie and friend.

Margaret Gabler at the New School for Social Research. Vicki began to come to life there under her tutelage.

Pat Vitiello, for taking wonderful care of my son, Nate, while I revised this novel before publication.

Thanks to the School of American Ballet for allowing me to observe classes.

And finally, a salute to Mikhail Baryshnikov, whose dancing inspired this and who remains one of the great artists of the century. I'm sure glad he decided to defect.

Chapter One

Here are some things I know about him. His full name is Mikhail Nikolaievich Baryshnikov. His friends call him Misha. He was born in Riga, Latvia, in 1947. He has four kids. He has two dogs. He's never been married. He defected to America right after a performance with the Kirov Ballet in 1974. He has blue eyes. He used to be able to do *eleven* pirouettes from one preparation. No one else could do that.

Here's another thing I know that nobody else knows. I love him more than anything in the world. When I'm not in dance class, I lie on my bed and write his name over and over in my diary. Misha. Misha. Misha. Misha and Vicki. Vicki Baryshnikov. Misha and Vicki Forever. I've been in love with him since last year when I first rented *The Turning Point*, that movie he was in a long time ago, before I was born. I've probably rented it thirty times since then. I've been doing ballet since I was eight (I'm fourteen now), but I never saw all it could be until I saw him. My favorite part of the movie is that part at the end when he's dancing *Don Quixote* and he comes flying from the wings, leaping across the stage like an angel. Then he stops and slides one leg out and does all those pirouettes without any effort, without any visible preparation, like it's natural, like it's what God means for him to be doing. Maybe it is. I don't usually think about God much, but Misha makes me think about things like that. Someone so beautiful, so perfect. How could he just have been born the same as I was? I don't get it.

I dream all the time of just being one-quarter as good. He's old, I know. And he's never been with anybody black, I know. But when I see him, when I look at that movie or one of my books or magazines that he's in, I don't know. None of that seems to matter. Everything falls away but me and him, the curve of his throat, the way his body looks as he turns. The way I always want to look. If I could just get near that perfection, just to touch him. It would be like being in heaven. I know it.

I've never told anybody how I feel. People wouldn't understand. I don't even have the words

2

for it. But when I went to audition for the School of American Ballet last winter, and when I got into the summer program, all I could think was that I was going to be near the New York City Ballet, where he danced for a little while. Of course I was excited—SAB is the best ballet school in the country—but I kept thinking how I might touch a barre Misha touched or use a rosin box he used or maybe even see him on the street. He must still have an apartment in the city somewhere. And I'll be right near Lincoln Center every day. He must come around there sometimes, even though he doesn't dance much anymore.

I was thinking about him as we drove into the city. Knowing he'd been to a school like this in Russia—the Kirov—made me feel less scared, until my mother's voice cut into my thoughts. "Now, Vicki, you know how proud I am of you. You've just got to remember to hold your head up. Don't let them treat you with ignorance."

"I won't, Ma." God. She must have said this stuff to me about a million times since I got into the school. I know she's trying to help but she just makes me nervous. What if the other girls were mean? What if I was the worst dancer? I expected to be the only black person—I'm kind of used to it in a way—but I'm the best in my ballet school at home. I might not be the best here. I looked back out the window as my mother's voice went on.

Since she got a divorce from my dad a few months ago, it always feels like she's lecturing me. Sometimes it's like I have two tapes in my head. I'll be nodding and smiling and responding the way I'm supposed to but in my head is only Misha. At first, when Ma and Dad broke up, there was nothing in my head but the words "How can you do this to me?" I didn't really yell at them, but I felt that way all the time. Like they were doing it to me, no matter how much they said they weren't. But then I just started thinking of Misha all the time and it got easier not to see them, not to hear them.

It's been a little while since I've seen my dad. He teaches Afro-American studies at Rutgers and he's like Mr. Heritage. All we ever heard about from the time I was little was being proud to be who we are and all about black history and what great people we come from. I didn't mind that when I was little—I used to love to listen to him talk, hearing his stories about growing up in Georgia and working his way through school. Not anymore. I can hardly stand to look at either of them now; they can't even talk to each other. They still fight on the phone whenever he calls. I usually go hide out in my room when that happens. I'm glad I won't be around this summer to hear it.

My mom's voice faded away as I looked out the window. I didn't see the cars passing by. I saw myself in an airy studio with high windows and a little rosin box in the corner. I was older, taller, thinner. I wasn't my same old self; I was Vicki Harris, *ballerina*. My hair stayed neat and flat in its elegant French twist and I was good. Really good. Practicing by myself, whipping through a series of fouettés, when Misha appeared at the door. Gray T-shirt, black tights, ripped gray legwarmers. His hair was sticking up a little like he'd been running his hands through it. He came in and offered his hand, saying, "You must have someone to practice with, you know." My heart was pounding as he took my hand and then we were dancing together. Every step was perfect; he touched me as if I was precious and delicate. When it was over, he looked at me and said—

"Ma, how much longer till we get there? I'm boiling back here."

My sister Beth's voice pulled my attention back into the car. She's eleven and she's a big pain. She hates ballet even though she's got the perfect body for it—long-legged and skinny. But she won't even watch ballet on TV. She wants to be a me-

5

chanic when she grows up. "Dag, Beth. Will you quit kicking my seat? What are you trying to do, put me through the windshield?"

"Oh sorr-rry, Miss Queen of the Ballerinas. Didn't mean to disturb you."

I turned to give her a dirty look. Ma jumped in. "Now just stop it, both of you. I don't want to have to deal with this traffic and with your nonsense."

We both shut up. She had that tone in her voice that means business. Besides, we were almost there. I could still feel Misha's hand in mine.

Besides getting into SAB, the other great thing about coming to New York for the summer is that I get to stay with my Aunt Hannah on the Upper West Side. She's an actress and my mom's best friend from when they were little. They used to pretend they were sisters; that's why I call her my aunt. She has this perfect little church-girl face—hair in a neat straightened pageboy, even medium-brown skin—but then when she opens her mouth she's so funny and crazy. She dated Denzel Washington a long time ago, before he got famous. She says he looks a lot better now that his teeth are capped. She's always saying stuff like that. I love her. I wish I could be that wild. She says acting is hard, though. She's always auditioning and not working as much as she'd like to; she makes a lot

6

of commercials. She's read for a lot of movies but she hasn't gotten that big part yet. She had a part on a soap opera but her character found out that she had an evil twin who hated her and they got into a battle to the death on a rooftop and they both fell off. Aunt Hannah says they just didn't want to pay her what she was worth and that they didn't know how to handle a black story line.

One time, before my father left, she came to visit us and I got her to come to school one day and talk about acting. "Most of being an actor is keeping on when you lose," she said in her speech. But she sure didn't seem like a loser. You would have thought she was Whitney Houston or something the way everybody was acting. I was a celebrity myself for a few days after her visit—all these girls I don't even know came up to me saying stuff like "I can't believe your aunt played Sophia. I was so sad when she died. You're lucky to have somebody famous in the family." But then things went back to normal; I hardly know anybody at school, really. I have so many dance classes and with my homework and all, I don't have that much time to see friends. So I don't have that many friends.

We were driving up Broadway now. Montclair isn't far from the city, so I'd been here before. But now that I was going to stay for six weeks, it seemed different. The heat shimmering off the

7

pavement made everyone's feet look wavy. They all looked like they knew where they were going and exactly what they were going to do when they got there. It seemed like if I looked long enough Misha would just walk right past the car and I could jump out and introduce myself.

Aunt Hannah's building has a big lobby with dingy black-and-white tiles on the floor and the elevators off to the side, one for each half of the building. It smells like all the paint that's been put on the walls and all the people who have stood looking into their mailboxes there for years and years. Her apartment is small but she's spent a lot of time fixing it up. She has mudcloth and African sculptures everywhere and pretty furniture made out of that light-colored wood. It's the kind of apartment I want when I get older. She didn't even wait for us to get up in the elevator; she was standing in the hall waiting for us as we got off. "Oh, I'm so happy to see you guys," she said over and over as she hugged and kissed first me, then Beth, then Ma. She gave Ma an extra-long hug, then stood holding her shoulders for a minute. "How you doing, Alicia?"

My mother bit her lip. "I'm hanging in there, Hannah. It's rough, but I'm hanging." Aunt Hannah pulled her in to hug her again. Beth scowled and pushed past them. My heart started beating

8

really fast—I had this vision of yelling at them for a minute—but then I just pushed past them into the living room too. Ever since my parents got divorced, Ma's been so weepy. You ask her the simplest thing and she gets all choked up. I feel like she did this; she's the one who wanted a divorce. Now she's got to live with it. I don't feel sorry for her.

Aunt Hannah led us all into the apartment and stood with her arm around Ma for a minute, looking at me. I don't think she noticed the way Beth and I had stomped in. "Vicki, I'm so happy to have you stay with me this summer," she said. "And I'm so proud of you for getting into this school."

"You know they only picked sixteen girls out of more than two hundred," said my mom.

They both beamed at me. I didn't know where to look. Finally Beth broke in. "Can we knock off the mutual admiration society and go eat? I'm starved."

For once I was glad she interrupted. I hate being fussed over. I know it's great that I got into this school, but what if I fall right on my face? They haven't even considered that. But it could happen.

Aunt Hannah laughed. "I guess you're right, Beth. Even ballerinas need to eat. Okay, let me just show you your room right quick, Vicki. Wanna see it, Beth?" She led us into a tiny room down the hall. There was a futon sofa bed in the corner, already unfolded. It almost filled the room. I threw my suitcase on the bed and Beth immediately flopped next to it to see how the bed was. When we were both little, whenever we went on a family vacation, we used to take a running start across the room and jump onto the hotel bed. We called it "testing it out." "This feels good, Vick," Beth said, splayed out like a starfish. "It's a little bit hard but you can get used to it. I can't believe you get to stay here all summer. Are you gonna go up in the Statue of Liberty?"

"I don't know. Probably not. I'm gonna be pretty busy."

"I wanna do that the next time we come." She threw herself across my suitcase, laughing. I shoved her out of the way, but I wasn't really mad. She looked at me for a minute. "You're lucky, coming here." Her voice changed. "Do you think Ma and Dad are going to fight all summer?"

"I don't know. I think they might be getting a little better. Maybe it'll be okay."

"I hope so," Beth sighed. "I hate listening to them. I wish you were still going to be around."

I sat next to her on the bed. It's weird. Sometimes I just hate her. Like this afternoon in the car,

I wanted to strangle her. But then other times I wouldn't trade her for anything. I feel like I have to watch out for her. "It'll be okay. You can call me anytime you want."

She looked up at me. "Thanks, Vick." She scooted off the bed. "Come on, you can unpack later. I'm starving to death."

When I was little, I remember asking my mother if people in New York ever went to bed. She laughed and said no, not really. It wasn't very late when we went out to dinner but I was thinking about that as we walked along. There were just so many people everywhere. No trees, no grass, just people, going places, eating ice cream, talking loud like if they lowered their voices, they'd never be heard from again. It smelled hot, like melted ice cream and sweat and old pee. There was this couple that both looked like models walking arm in arm; then there were about ten boys skateboarding in a big pack. We walked past this dirty, filthy person—I couldn't even tell if it was a man or a woman—huddled in a doorway under a blanket. Beth saw him and jumped, grabbing my hand. She looked at me quickly to see if it was okay; I didn't mind. I was a little scared too.

Aunt Hannah took us to this very fancy place

where a lot of actors hang out. It was nice, although at first I was worried that everything would be really fattening and there'd be nothing I could eat. Once we got there Beth got very excited because there was some guy that's been on *90210* sitting in the back. I have class Wednesday nights so I never see the show. One time I was in the bathroom with Rachel and Sharon, these two girls I know a little bit, and Rachel started raving about Luke Perry, how cute he is and how she'd just *die* to talk to him or something. I turned and said, "Who is he? A new kid?" They both looked at me like I'd just grown horns out of my head. Sharon said, "You don't know who Luke Perry is?" I was wishing I'd never said anything so I just shook my head. They looked at each other and then they told me all about the show and Rachel showed me a little picture of Luke Perry that she had in her wallet. I could hear them laughing after I left the bathroom. They make me sick. Luke Perry. Who cares? He's nothing compared to Misha. But I can't explain it. I don't even try.

Aunt Hannah was asking me a question above the clatter of the restaurant. "So tell me again how many classes you'll be taking?"

"I'll be taking ten a week. Two classes a day except on Wednesday and one on Saturday."

"You sure have more focus than I did at your

age." She turned to Ma. "Can you imagine being that busy at fourteen?"

"No, I really can't." Ma was smiling, but I knew underneath she was a little worried. Right before my dad moved out, when I went up to six classes a week from four, she sat me down.

"Vicki, you've gotten very serious about dancing. Do you know everything it involves? It's a hard, hard life."

"I know, Ma," I answered, "but I really want to try. I'm good at it and I love dancing. You know I do."

She sighed. "I know it. I guess it's just hard for me to see you work so hard at your age. You should be having fun."

"I am," I said. She didn't look like she believed me.

It's hard. There are moments when I can almost feel it, like the first time I did a double pirouette and I was spinning around and I didn't get dizzy and I didn't fall and I felt for just a second what it would be like to really dance. It was the best feeling I ever had. It was so far away from everything else I never wanted to come back. That's why I keep doing it. To try and get that feeling again. At those times, it's not even so much about how I look as about how I feel. Like I could fly. Like I'm part of everything beautiful in the world. I'm not even thinking—I'm only feeling. It's just so hard to get to that place.

Beth's voice cut into my thoughts. "I don't know how you can stand it, Vick," she said. "It smells so sweaty in your dance school in the summer. And you could be outside doing stuff. I'd go crazy."

"Yeah, I know. But this is what it takes. It's the only way to get good."

"I guess. I wouldn't do it, though."

"I know you wouldn't, peanut-head. That's why I'm doing it."

It was about nine-thirty by the time we finished dinner and headed back. Beth drooped a little and held Ma's hand. Aunt Hannah must have been able to tell I was tired because she smiled and put her arm around me. We all walked into the lobby without talking.

"We've got to get back, Hannah. We'll be up in a couple of weeks, and then you and I are going to have to really talk," said Ma, smiling. I can imagine what she was like when she was my age when she's with Aunt Hannah. She seems softer and she laughs more. Since my dad left she hardly laughs at all. Her eyes are always on the verge of tears.

People say I look like her. I used to love to hear that; I don't so much anymore. But she is really pretty, with perfect chocolate-brown skin and a

14

short Afro. She wanted me to wear my hair that way, but last year I insisted on growing it out and having it straightened so I could put it in a bun. We fought every day for two weeks over it.

"Vicki, don't you see?" she would say. "The hair you have, we've been taught to hate, to try to hide for years and years. Centuries. You can't just straighten it like it doesn't matter."

"But Mom, ballet dancers have straight hair. That's all there is to it. And I'm gonna be a ballet dancer so I have to have straight hair."

She sighed. "Do you ever think about why ballet dancers all have straight hair?" I just looked at her like she was crazy. "I didn't think so. Vicki, they didn't even used to let us dance ballet. For years, they said our butts were too big, our legs were too long. And they still won't accept our hair the way it grows out of our heads. Don't you see why this upsets me?"

"Ma, I know, I know. You've been talking about this stuff ever since I was little. But I don't see why what I do with my hair makes a difference. I have to straighten it, Ma. If I'm ever gonna make it, I've gotta look like everybody else."

She looked like she was going to cry. I ran out of the room. The next day, she came into my room and said, "I guess it's up to you. But I'm not taking you to the beauty parlor. Hannah's coming

15

down this weekend. She'll take you." My hair felt funny to me at first after I did it. It was so limp and soft—but then I got so I liked how it felt. Ma wouldn't look me in the eye for a week after I did it. But now I guess she's used to it. It goes up pretty well but I have to put a lot of gel in it to get it to stay flat against my head. But now I look more like everybody else in class. My hair does, anyway.

That was the hardest thing when I started studying ballet. I'd look at myself in the mirror with all the other girls and I was always the first thing I saw. My own dark skin, my fuzzy hair, my long brown legs. I started feeling like I just stuck out so much. And then one of our teachers, Mrs. Gore, was always talking about how ballet, especially the corps work, was based on an "absolute visual harmony" and then looking quickly at me and away. What was I supposed to think? At first I got mad but then I got worried that she was right. It wasn't long after that that I started straightening my hair. And Mrs. Gore nodded with approval the first time she saw it.

That was all a long time ago. Now, as my mom and Beth got ready to leave, she pulled me toward her and hugged me real tight. "You take care of yourself. Make sure you eat and wrap your feet up right before class. I'll call you every day. You let me know if there are any problems, any problems at all."

"I will, Ma."

"I'm going to miss you, Vicki. But I know you'll be all right. You're a special girl. Don't forget that."

"I won't."

"Bye, Vick," Beth said. "Are you sure I can't borrow your black jacket?"

"No, you cannot. Geez, Beth. Can't you be normal for one second?"

"I *am* normal," she said. She looked serious for a minute. "This is really weird, but I'm going to miss you bossing me around. The house will be so quiet without you."

"Yeah." I paused. "I'll probably miss you too, kind of. Take care of yourself. And stay away from that jacket."

"Yes ma'am." They walked down the block to the car and drove off. My eyes stung. Aunt Hannah put her arm around me. "Don't worry. I'll be looking out for you," she said.

That night, I lay in my strange new bed, looking out at the silvery streetlight. I could feel the wooden slats, even though the futon was thick, and the sheets didn't smell like home. I could hear Aunt Hannah moving around in the living room, and beyond that, I could hear people talking on the street. A siren raced by, a police car or an ambulance. I sat up, feeling my heart pound. I thought of Misha, lying in some huge bed in a beautiful apartment in another part of the city. Maybe he was looking out at the streetlight too. Thinking of his home back in Russia. I could almost feel his hand in mine. It would be warm and a little bit sweaty. He'd have rosin on the tips of his fingers from the barre. I'd feel it as we worked together on a variation. Or as he pushed the straps of my leotard down to kiss my shoulders. Like he did to Leslie Browne in *The Turning Point*.

He took my hand as we finished dancing and pulled me close to him. I was looking straight into those perfect blue eyes. The air was very still around us.

"You dance very well," he said, smiling, not letting me go. "Do you do other things as well?"

"I . . . I guess."

"Well, I'd like to find out. Have dinner with me tonight? After the performance?"

"I'd love to . . . love to."

"Then you will. Around eleven. You are in the corps of *Etudes* tonight, no?"

"Yes, yes I am."

"Well, I have *Push Comes to Shove* after that and then we go. All right?"

"All right."

18

He turned to leave. Halfway to the door he stopped and said, "Try to keep your left shoulder from dropping when you turn to the left. It'll help you keep your balance." And then he was gone.

I fell asleep watching him go. When I woke up, all I could remember was his hand touching mine.

Chapter Two

Aunt Hannah didn't have a job the next day so she rode the subway with me to school. "I can't do this with you every day but you can't afford to take cabs all the time and you ought to learn how to do this yourself. It's part of being a real New Yorker," she said. I hadn't been on the subway since I was four, before we moved to Montclair.

Going down into the subway station was like walking into a wall of solid heat. Someone had sucked every bit of oxygen out and left only the smell of too many bodies. Aunt Hannah laughed when she saw my expression. "You never get used to it. But it's the only way to travel around here. And the trains are all air-conditioned these days. You should have been here five years ago before they overhauled them. Then it was *really* foul."

She got me a map and tokens and explained

that I would be taking the one train from Ninety-sixth Street downtown to Sixty-sixth, the Lincoln Center stop. The train was cool and nearly empty except for about six girls about my age who sat across from us. They were all black too and they were wearing big earrings, superbaggy jeans and sweatshirts and being really loud. One girl carried a baby wearing little Air Jordans and a hat with a pot leaf and the word *Blunt* on it. I couldn't figure out what they were talking about because they all kept laughing and yelling at once. It seemed to be about some guy named Pookey that they all knew. They weren't talking about me—they weren't even thinking about me—but I felt uncomfortable anyway. Girls like that always make me feel weird. But I kind of admire the way they don't care what anyone thinks either. My mom works with pregnant teenagers in Newark and she sees a lot of girls like them.

They all got off after a couple of stops. The girl with the baby carried him off the train by one arm. My mom always freaks when she sees people do that; she says it could hurt the baby. I didn't say anything, though; my mom will talk to strangers about stuff like that, but I get too mortified. I just can't.

I felt very proper, sitting there with my hair caught up in a bun. I know I'm supposed to feel

21

proud and strong about being black but I don't really always feel that way. Like when I see girls like that, I feel a little embarrassed. I mean, it's supposed to be like my dad always said, that we all share the same oppression. But I don't feel like my life is much like those girls'. Am I just lucky? If I lived where they lived, would I be like that, all loud and crazy? It makes me feel very strange to think about it.

But I didn't think about it for long. All of a sudden, Aunt Hannah was motioning for me to get off and we were at the school. I thought I was nervous when I auditioned, but I was a regular ice cube compared to how I felt now. I rubbed my dance bag and felt the smooth surface of the old *Vanity Fair* that I carry with me everywhere. It has a cover story on Misha. It helped a little to know it was there.

When we got into the school there was an unbelievable crush of noise. My heart was pounding like I'd just finished a really hard combination, and I couldn't breathe. We made our way up to the desk and Aunt Hannah registered me with the woman who sat there. There were squealing girls everywhere. The woman at the desk was grandmotherly but she looked kind of frantic. Four girls and their mothers were asking her questions all at the same time. All the girls were blond and tall.

One of them stood easily on pointe, leaning on the desk a little. I felt sick. Then Aunt Hannah put her hands on my shoulders and turned me around to face her. "Okay, Vicki. This is it. You're on your own now. You've got my phone number and you know how to get home, right?"

"Right."

"I know you're scared, honey, but it's okay. This is everything that you've worked for. And once you get in there and show them your stuff, it'll all be okay. You'll be dancing. That's what you want, isn't it?"

I nodded, but I still felt sick. She kissed me quickly, gave me a big hug and a shove toward the dressing rooms and left. I felt the way I did when I was eight and got lost in the mall. But I headed toward the dressing rooms anyway, checking to make sure that my hair wasn't sticking straight out from the sides of my head the way it sometimes does.

The room smelled of new paint and sweat. The carpet was nubbly no-color industrial stuff, just like every studio dressing room I'd ever been in. And like every dressing room I'd been in, there were mirrors everywhere. One thing about ballet, you're never out of sight of yourself. But I'd never seen dancers like the girls gathered there. Thin, so thin, and all so sure of themselves. They wrapped

23

their toes with lamb's wool to cushion them and keep them from bleeding and sewed pointe shoes and chattered like they'd all known each other for a million years. Everybody's hair went up perfectly and their legs stretched on for days. I have a good extension and a lot of height to my jumps but I would give anything for longer legs. Everybody here was like some kind of racehorse. My stomach felt like a ball of iron was in it and my hands, when I went to tie my shoes, were shaking a little. I sat down next to a girl with shiny blond hair and small pearl earrings. When she looked up, I could see her eyes were the color of the sea in a postcard. She smiled a little and then slid to the floor in a full split. "My name's Debbie Turner," she said. "Is this your first day?"

"Yeah." I pulled my new slippers on carefully, feeling inside to see if the innersole was loose. Then I slid off the bench a little ways from her and got into my best split, leaning over my extended leg.

"It's my first day too," she said. "I'm a little nervous."

"Me too," I confessed. I didn't know what to say after that, so I pretended to be very caught up in stretching out. She didn't say anything else either, just slid out of her split, settled a small pink sweater over her shoulders and said, "See you later," as she walked out. I watched her go, listening to the voices babble around me and feeling this weird impulse to run after her, or run out of the room.

"Did you see what she did to her hair this year?"

"I don't know. I think they're only gonna take the girls that look like Darci for the company this year."

"My knees are killing me but I . . ."

"Damn, I'm glad I'm not the only chip in this cookie." A laughing voice very close to my ear this time. I turned around to face a pretty, dark-skinned girl whose hair was cut in a supershort Afro. She wore small gold hoops in her ears. I couldn't believe she didn't have her hair straightened. "I'm Stacey Rogers. What's your name?"

"Um . . . I'm Vicki Harris. Did you come in late? I didn't see you when I got here."

"I guess we both kind of stand out, huh? I just got here. I was over in the corner. What's your first class?"

"Intermediate technique. I don't have pointe till this afternoon."

"Cool. We're in the same class. Guess we should get down there. Come on." She grabbed my hand and pulled me after her. I didn't even have time to think.

LELAND HIGH SCHOOL

The studio was twice the size of my studio at home, but except for the size it was familiar. The piano in the corner with cans of diet Coke and sheets of music all over it. The girls standing with their legs up on the barre or resting in splits, all dressed alike in navy leotards and pink tights. I saw that girl Debbie counting to herself and practicing glissades in the corner. She looked good. Everybody was eyeing everybody else, trying to see who had the skinniest legs, the longest neck, the purest extension. Once class got started, things would begin to organize themselves according to who had it and who might not. Every class I'd ever been in was the same way. It made the air thick with nervousness, giggles flying tightly through the air. We knew how it worked but we were all a little scared anyway.

The teacher came in and we all turned to look at her. My breath caught in my throat. She had danced with Misha during that season he was with NYCB. I knew it. From one of my old dance magazines. Oh my God. I stood up a little straighter, tried to make my neck longer. I couldn't believe it. She was everything a dancer ought to be. Tall and razor thin with a long, long neck and long legs. Her dark hair was caught up in a neat bun with just a few wisps trailing down the back of her

26

neck. She walked to stand in front of the mirrors and called out, "My name is Melanie Reinman. Should you need to address me, you'll call me Miss Reinman. Hands on the barre, please. We're about to begin."

It was the hardest class I'd ever had. Once we got started I couldn't even worry about her and Misha, I just had to concentrate. The barre was okay but the combinations across the floor were so fast. Piqués into châinés into arabesques until I thought I would faint. I caught sight of myself in the mirror once—my hair was sticking up, I was gnawing on my lip, I was so nervous that nothing was flowing at all. But I got through it. And I didn't fall on my face. That was okay for my first class, I guess. But I didn't get any corrections from Miss Reinman. Even though it was our first day, some other girls did. I've got to do better next class. If they don't correct you, it means they think there's no hope.

After class, we all lined up to thank Miss Reinman. Back home at my school in New Jersey, we would just applaud at the end of class but here, the girls that had been here before went quickly toward her at the end of class, standing in a neat line and shaking her hand. She looked at me with a big, open smile—her first of the day—and said

"You're welcome" as I thanked her. That made me feel better but I still wished that she'd given me a couple of corrections. We all walked back up to the dressing room, smelling of sweat and rosin, people talking about what class they had next and stopping at the soda machine to get diet Cokes. There was a machine with some snacks in it—nuts and candy and things like that—but nobody went to that one.

Once I sat down in the dressing room, that girl, Stacey, dragged her bag over and sat next to me to change. "So what'd you think?"

"It was okay." I didn't want her to think that I couldn't handle it.

"Well, it was kickin' my black ass. Back home, I'm the best in my school, but this is something else. It really didn't bother you?"

I looked directly at her for the first time. She reminded me of those girls on the subway a little bit, like she didn't care what other people thought of her. You could tell by the way she wore her hair and the way she looked at you without blinking. But she was a dancer too. So she didn't scare me. "Well, maybe a little," I admitted.

She laughed. "I thought so. Listen, there's a Wendy's two blocks over and we have time before class. You wanna go?"

"They have a salad bar, right?"

"Yeah, sure. God forbid we should eat real food. You ready? Let's go."

Outside it was sunny and sticky warm. The big plaza sparkled and was filled with people rushing around. A group of actory-looking guys sat on the edge of the fountain, eating hot dogs and pushing their hair out of their eyes. I blinked a little at the light—the studio we'd been in didn't have any windows. Those were all for the most advanced classes and the company. My legs were a little sore but in a good way. Stacey chattered on about the class and about Miss Reinman—"That girl is hard as nails. She won't be cutting us any slack. I can tell already."

"Well, she used to be one of the best dancers in the company, back in the seventies. She's used to giving hard classes," I said.

"Tell me something I don't know," said Stacey, grinning. "I guess you gotta be hard to last that long in the company. And she has a nice smile."

"She danced with Baryshnikov, you know," I said, wondering if Stacey could hear in my voice how that made me feel.

"Oh yeah? Cool. He was great." That's all she said. I didn't go into the Misha thing. Stacey and I had just met, after all.

By the time we got to the restaurant, we had discussed everybody's technique in class (good but

29

a few of the girls were too skinny), and our own movements in class (we were both nervous and thought we hadn't done as well as we could).

"So where are you from?" she asked once we got settled with our salads.

"I'm from New Jersey. How about you?"

"Chicago. I've been studying since I was eight. I'd really love to make it into Dance Theatre of Harlem one day but my mom made me go on the audition for this school. She said it was a chance I couldn't pass up and if I was good enough to get in here, I'd have a foundation nobody could ever take away from me. I guess she's right but sometimes I get tired of being around so many white girls all the time. This is just like my school at home."

I didn't know what to say. It was like my school at home too but that's just how ballet is. That's how it seemed like it should be to me sometimes. I mean, I can't really imagine those girls on the subway going to the ballet. Even my own sister doesn't like it. So why should people have to do what they might not like? I mean, I like it but lots of other black people don't. What's the big deal? I never thought of joining Dance Theatre of Harlem. I wanted to be where Misha had been. To be someplace where he might see me. But I

30

couldn't say all that to Stacey. I'd just met her. So I said, "Yeah, mine too. I guess you just have to get used to it, though. I mean, ballet's just like that."

"Mmm. Well, I get sick of it sometimes. All my friends at home that don't dance are black, and then I come to dance class all the time and I'm the only one. I hate it. But I love dancing and I don't want to give it up. The whole thing sucks." She took a pull of her diet Coke.

I'd never heard anybody talk like this before. I'd thought some of it but I never knew how to say it. I never had anybody to say it to. All my friends at home were white—it bothered my dad but he never said anything. I could just tell. And besides, I don't know, it's like I *am* proud but it's in this really abstract way. My dad made me and Beth watch *Eyes on the Prize* back when it was on TV a while ago. It was all about the civil rights movement. I didn't want to watch it—I had a lot of homework and I needed to do some stretching but he said we had to, so I sat there in a split, hating him, feeling mad. Martin Luther King was cool. I liked that part, the sound of his voice. But he's dead now. And when I look around my ballet school, I don't see anyone like me. When I look around the world, I don't see anyone like Martin Luther King. I'm proud of what he did, I know it

31

helped me and other black people, but I don't totally see what it has to do with me now. No one's kept me from eating in a restaurant or anything. I know I'm not supposed to think that. But that's how I feel. Everything that's important to me doesn't have much to do with the color of my skin. And hardly anybody black does the things I love to do, like ballet. It all gets to be a jumble in my head. I can't say any of it. So I just sat there. Maybe Stacey could tell I didn't know what to say because after a minute, she said, "So what about you? When did you start studying?"

"When I was eight. My parents brought us into the city to see *The Nutcracker* and I just lost it. I begged my mom so much she finally found someplace where I could take classes. I was driving her crazy. When I made the cut in this audition, I was so happy I thought I'd die."

Stacey smiled. "Yeah. I know I'm complaining but I felt the same way. Have you started doing any partnering at home?"

"No, not yet. I've just been on pointe for about six months. I don't know. I'm kind of excited about partnering, but then when I look at some of the guys in my ballet school at home—yeesh."

"I know what you mean. Do I want some guy's clammy hands all over me?"

Misha's maybe. These other guys can forget it, though, I thought. "I guess I'm gonna find out this afternoon."

"Are you in adagio this afternoon too?" Stacey asked.

"Yeah."

"Thank God. I'll know someone in there. How many other classes are you taking?" she asked.

"Nine. How about you?"

"Nine. I guess we'll be in a lot of the same ones."

"Cool."

We talked some more and by the time lunch was done, I decided that I liked Stacey. She was kind of wild but in a good way. And she was serious about dancing. I could tell by the cool way that she talked about the technique of everyone in class. She was pretty good herself too—though there were quite a few girls there that were better than both of us. I was gonna need a friend here and she would be a good one to have. My dad would be thrilled. I was finally making friends with somebody black. Then Stacey poked me in the ribs, jarring me out of my thoughts. "Girl, did you see that guy behind the counter?"

"What guy?"

"That one. There." She pointed at a guy,

maybe fifteen, with skin so dark it looked polished and big brown eyes. He was taking somebody's order. "Yeah. What about him?"

"He was *seriously* checking you out, Vicki. Just a minute ago."

"Yeah, right."

"No, he really was. He's cute too."

"Yeah, well, I don't have time for all that. Besides, he works in a Wendy's, for God's sake. I can't deal with that."

She looked at me for a minute. "Well, you do what you want," she said finally.

She's got to be kidding. I'm taking ten dance classes a week, at the best ballet school in New York City, where I might run into Misha at any minute, and she's pointing out some guy in a fast-food restaurant for me? Hello? I don't think so. I was worried she thought I was being a snob. I didn't mean to be. But even if he was looking at me, what would we talk about? I bet he's never even been to the ballet.

I forgot about that as soon as we got back to school, though. It was time for adagio. All the boys were lined up on one side of the room, resting their legs on the barre and nervously talking. All the girls lined up on the other like there was some invisible electric fence down the middle of the room. I was so nervous I didn't even know

34

what to look at; I just kept fussing with my hair and tying and retying my pointe shoes. Stacey asked me to help her stretch and acted like we were the only ones in the room. I think she was trying not to show that she was nervous too.

The room fell silent when the teacher came in; a man this time, wearing regular pants and a shirt and soft jazz shoes. "I'm Mr. Mazo, this is beginning adagio and yes, you're going to have to touch each other in this class." We all laughed and took our places at the barre. The barre was the same exercises as usual; that was easy. Going to the center was the hard part.

Mr. Mazo looked us over quickly and paired us up with guys about our height, telling us that it was polite to introduce ourselves but not to get into long conversations; I got a skinny blond guy named Josh who was so nervous he was shaking a little. I was like, God, what if we have to do lifts today; this guy's totally going to drop me. But I got lucky. We just worked on supported pirouettes and arabesques. It felt funny to be doing that stuff with someone; we're all usually so alone in class. It didn't feel the way I thought it would with Misha. With him, I bet it would be like being on a cloud. His hands on my waist, supporting me, his breath on the back of my neck, both of us looking in the mirror, counting the beats, breathing with one heart. With Josh it was sweaty and a little scary. I could smell potato chips on his breath when I spun around to face him. His hand, when I took it, was damp and soft. But he didn't drop me and I didn't fall. When class was over and Josh and I thanked each other (Mr. Mazo said that was what we were supposed to do), we smiled a little bit. "You're a good dancer," he said, looking at the floor.

"So are you." He was really just okay, but you can't say that to somebody. Not right to their face. We decided to pair off again next class. I'd heard some older girls at my school at home say that it's easier to stick with the same partner when you first start adagio. I didn't feel as bad as I was afraid I would once it was all over. But I felt a long way from flying.

Chapter Three

When I first fell in love with Misha, I would sometimes say to myself, "This is a little weird. He's a lot older than you. And you don't really know him." But that's faded as I've learned more about him. I feel like I do know him now.

I've imagined going out with him for the first time so many times, I know it by heart. All the other girls in the corps tease me about having a hot date but I just smile mysteriously. When I meet him at his dressing room, he smiles and takes my hand. We walk to his car through a lot of twisty hallways behind Lincoln Center. We don't talk for a few minutes; then he says to me with an odd, shy look, "I go this way a couple of times a week. There are always people waiting if I go out the stage door."

When he says that, I remember the knot of

anxious-looking women who are there after every performance, hoping just to see him, to get him to sign something, look at them a moment. I close my eyes for a second, making fists at my sides. *I'm with him. I can touch him if I want to.* A miracle.

He doesn't say much while we drive to the restaurant. I watch him smoke. He holds the cigarette the way a French person would, making each draw seem graceful, perfect. After a while, at a stoplight, he turns to me and says, "What are you thinking?"

I say, without even trying to stop the words, "I'm thinking how beautiful you are."

He smiles slightly but his eyes are serious and considering. "You know, you are a very interesting girl. Not everybody would say something like that very easily."

"Well, I'm not everybody."

"No, you're not." He turns back to the road, still grinning a little.

That's how it always goes in my mind. Whenever I think about being with him like that, I feel like I can't breathe; it would be so perfect; I'd be so perfect then. I'd always say the right thing. Not like real life where I always think of the right thing to say when it's too late. Or I think of it but then I'm too afraid to say it. In my head, with Misha, we're like in some romantic movie or something.

38

But I bet being with him would be like that. How could it not be? He's so perfect.

My dad came up to see me this Saturday. My mom and he decided it would be best if he didn't come with us when she and Beth brought me up. They didn't ask me. I didn't want him to come with us—they'd have fought the whole way—but they didn't even ask me what I wanted. I went to see him the weekend after I got into SAB. It was the first time I'd seen him in about two weeks—we're supposed to see him every week but with my Saturday classes, I don't always make it. He was so excited I thought he was going to start jumping up and down. You'd think he'd gotten into SAB himself. He's still living in New Jersey, but he got an apartment closer to Rutgers. It's small. It's nice, I guess. He has a lot of framed posters and that old picture of Malcolm X and Martin Luther King that used to hang in our house. It made me sad to see it there. I was used to seeing it in our hall.

He took me to a really fancy restaurant for lunch, and kept squirming around, looking like he wanted a cigarette the whole time. He quit smoking a year ago.

"So how're the classes going?"

"Good, Dad. I really love it."

"That's great, honey. You know how proud I am of you."

"I know. How's your school going?"

"Oh, summer school's all right. The kids don't want to be there and that makes it harder but it's okay." He paused like he didn't know what else to say. "You don't need any money or anything, do you?"

"No, I'm fine. Really. Aunt Hannah's looking out for me and I don't have time to go shopping or anything anyway." Ever since they got divorced, all he does is ask me if I need money. He's only been to see me dance a few times—even with him being all excited about me going to SAB. I think he was more excited just because he knew it was really famous. He doesn't like ballet that much— "Alvin Ailey, that's the only dance I've ever really liked," he said to me once. He knows I love it but he doesn't understand it. Before he moved out, sometimes I'd catch him looking at me sitting in a split or sewing my toe shoes. He'd have this look on his face like I was a stranger. Then he'd just smile and walk away. It made me feel really weird.

"I'd sure love to see you dance up here sometime. Are you going to have any recitals or anything?" His voice cut into my thoughts.

"No, Dad. They don't have recitals at a place like SAB. It's too big. Some of these people will go on to join the company." I paused. "They're the best."

"Well, that just means you're one of the best. Don't forget it."

"I won't."

He fiddled with the empty soda glass in front of him for a minute. "So is there any way I can see you dance up here?"

"Well, there's an open class at the end of the summer, but . . ."

"But your mother and sister are coming." His eyes turned dark and his voice flattened out as he stopped fiddling with the glass. "Well. I'll see you another time then." He looked away and signaled for the waiter.

I hadn't eaten much but everything I ate just turned into a hard ball in my stomach. My eyes stung.

We didn't say any more as we walked out of the restaurant. He went to hail a cab to take him to the train station but before one stopped, he gave me a big, bone-crusher hug. His rough jacket scratched my cheek. He brushed my cheek gently and said, "Take care of yourself, baby girl." Most times I would have said, "I'm not a baby," and laughed. But now I couldn't speak. I just watched the space where his cab had been for a while after he was gone.

The day he moved out, I sat in my room for a long time. I had that *Vanity Fair* with Misha on

41

the cover on the bed with me and I kept running my fingers over his eyes, the curve of his cheek, like if I did it long enough, Misha would just appear before me and make this end. I could hear my father throwing things into boxes and bags, his voice muttering "goddamnit, goddamnit" over and over. Sometimes he'd drop something and swear even louder. My mom didn't make a sound. Beth didn't come into my room. It was like me and the sound of him moving were the only sounds in the universe. Finally he came in, Beth trailing behind him. He made us both sit on the bed. "You girls know that I'm leaving today. I hope you know that I love you both." His voice cracked. "I love you both very much. But I can't stay here. I don't know. When you're older you might understand." He took a long breath and looked away from us, out the window. "But you probably won't." He turned and left without another word, without touching either of us. My hand rested on Misha's face. Beth sat beside me without moving, tears running down her cheeks. My mom still didn't come out of her room. We both watched his car drive away until it turned the corner and we couldn't see it anymore.

I don't know why they broke up. They never said anything that made any sense. They kept saying it wasn't anybody's fault, that they just couldn't live together anymore. But that's what parents always say. I think that's what they tell you to say in the books about how to not ruin your kids' lives when you get divorced. But they did ruin my life. It felt like that at first. Dancing was all I could stand to do. I didn't look so great in class either then, but I had to get out of the house. Looking at Ma, I just wanted to hit her. I wanted to scream at her and ask why she made him move out if it made her so sad to do it. She kept staring at Beth and me like we were made of gold or something and it made me really mad. If she thought we were so great, why couldn't she and Dad work something out? Neither of them has anybody else. They used to be happy. There must have been some way to go back to that. If you really love someone, then you should try as hard as you can to stay together. You shouldn't make them move out. That's what I think.

During the days after my father left, my mom was really busy, always running around, coming up with projects for us to do and smiling so much that her cheeks looked strained. It's like she knew it was all her fault and was trying to make up for it. After about a month and a half of this, I finally took a deep breath and said to her, "Mom, you don't have to try so hard to cheer us up. Maybe we just have to be sad for a while."

43

She smiled but looked sad at the same time and said, "I just hate for us all to be so unhappy. I want you both to know how much we love you."

I felt my face get hot. "I *know* that, Ma. But this really hurts. We can't just cover it up." I stopped talking. I was afraid I would cry.

She gave me a big hug, her eyes shiny, and said, "You know, you're right. I'm going to try to just let you kids feel how you feel about this and I will too. It's hard, I know. But we'll get through it."

After that, we didn't get so many pep talks. I didn't talk much at all to her, really. I thought about Misha all the time. I loved to read about when he defected in Toronto, all those years ago. How he had so many curtain calls that he couldn't get away and his friends were worried. How he ran, still wearing his stage makeup, to the car, past all the autograph hounds, running away from the KGB. In a weird way, it makes me feel like he'd understand about my parents and about dancing and about everything. He gave up everything he ever knew to come to America. Just ran away from all that was familiar because he knew that was the only way he could live. He knows what it's like to lose everything you thought you knew in a moment.

Chapter Four

Before I came to SAB, my mom talked a lot about how great it would be to be in New York for the summer. "When I lived there with Hannah right after I graduated, there wasn't anything we didn't do," she'd say. "We went to the Met and up in the Empire State Building, to Shakespeare in the Park. Oh, it was so much fun!" She'd be smiling and her eyes were all shiny just remembering it. But I knew it wouldn't be the way she remembered for me when I got there. And I was right. It's not like I didn't care that I was in New York—I loved the rush of it, the subways and the hot dog vendors and the buildings all reaching for the sky—but all I did was go from Hannah's house to class to Wendy's for lunch with Stacey to another class and then back to Hannah's house to bandage my bleeding toes and sew my toe shoes for tomorrow and have some yogurt and go to sleep. I didn't even have as much time to think about Misha as I wanted. I just hung on to the thought that by getting to be a better dancer, I was getting to be what he would want me to be, getting closer to him.

And I was getting better. I could see the muscles in my legs getting long and corded. Sometimes it even seemed like my neck was getting longer, like I was taller somehow. And like everybody else, I tried not to eat too much, mostly yogurt and salad and diet sodas. But it was never good enough. Like last week, I was picked to demonstrate a variation. I thought I'd die. It wasn't too hard—a couple of turns, a glissade—but getting picked to demonstrate is a big deal and I did it perfectly. For once, I was really dancing, a part of the music, liquid and free. I saw myself in the mirror like a stranger—tall, thin, honey brown, with long legs and an airy extension. Everyone's eyes were on me for those few seconds—even Ms. Reinman had a slight, approving smile. After class, Stacey hugged me. "Go on, girl. Show 'em that stuff." Then that girl Debbie came up to us and said to me, "You looked good today."

"Thanks," I said, still smiling. I could feel my thigh muscles humming. We all walked up to the dressing room together, rehashing class and trying to decide what Miss Reinman did when she wasn't teaching. Debbie and Stacey knew each other from the dorms—and we all knew Debbie. Not only was she really nice but she was the one person in class that everyone knew was going to go all the way. She had the perfect proportions, the extension, the speed—everything. Even though things went well today, I knew that I was on the short side and that they didn't go this way often enough for me to be sure. I mean, I'm determined to make it but sometimes I look in the mirror and what I see is good, but not quite good enough. My teacher back home told me once—"Vicki, you've got the spirit, and you're a talented dancer, but I don't know if you've got the body to make it into City Ballet. They like tall, tall girls. And there's just so many who want in." I cried off and on for three days after that, but it just made me work harder in class. When I got into SAB, she was one of the first people I told. I wanted to let her know that they thought I was good enough to go to their doggone school. She said she was pleased for me. I think she meant it.

I was in such a good mood from class that I invited Debbie to come have lunch with Stacey and me. I found out that she was from Ann Arbor, Michigan, and both her parents were professors. "They think this ballet thing is crazy," she said.

47

"They want me to go to college and become a professor or something like them. I haven't told them there's no way I'm going to college."

"Me either," I said. "My parents would wig if they knew. I'm just going to wait until it's closer." I paused. "And I guess I'll have to see if the company wants me." Debbie and Stacey both nodded but neither of them jumped in to say "Oh, they'll want you for sure." I was so happy that it didn't even bother me. That day, I knew that I could go as far as I wanted to.

The next day was the total opposite. I practically fell over when we tried to do pirouettes. Nobody laughed or anything—we're not supposed to—but my face was hot as I went to the back of the line to try again. I felt like everyone was looking at me again and thinking, *What's wrong with her? No consistency at all.* Miss Reinman moved the class along as though nothing at all had happened. Stacey stood next to me and muttered under her breath, "You think Darci Kistler never slipped in class? Shake it off, Vick. It happens to the best of them." I knew she was right but I moved like a stick figure for the whole rest of the hour. I couldn't turn off the voices in my head.

After, I told Stacey I wasn't hungry and she should go on and eat. She went off to the cafeteria with Debbie and some other girls who lived in the dorms with them. I went over to Wendy's by myself and just ordered a diet Coke. I really didn't feel like eating. I was sitting with it and staring out the window when that guy came by, busing tables. He *was* looking at me. I felt my face getting hot.

"Are you done with this?" he said, pointing at my tray.

"Yeah." He picked it up and then stood there for a minute. "I've seen you in here before," he finally said.

"I've been here before."

"You go to school around here?"

"No. I mean, yeah. I go to the ballet school over at Lincoln Center."

He smiled. He had a really pretty smile. "I thought so. But I wasn't sure. I don't see too many folks like us over there, you know what I'm sayin'?"

"Yeah. Well, that's where I go."

"A ballerina, huh? That's cool. What's your name, ballerina?"

"My name?"

He laughed. "Yeah. Most people I know have names. Mine's Michael Bowman. What's yours?"

"Vicki. Vicki Harris." Why was I even telling him this? He could be a serial killer, a con man, anything. I know my mom would not want me talking to strange boys in Wendy's. But he just kept standing there.

"Listen," he finally said, "are you in class all the time? I mean, I've seen you in here a lot. Maybe we could hang sometime?"

"Hang? You mean like do something together? Go out?"

"Yeah. Something like that." He was fiddling with the tray he'd picked up.

"I don't have much time for that kind of stuff," I said quickly.

"All right, then. I can take a hint."

"But maybe sometime. We could figure something out." I could not believe I said that. I didn't even think about it before it jumped out of my mouth. He smiled again and nodded. "Cool. I'll see you soon then."

As I walked back across the street to school, I couldn't get over myself. What was I thinking saying yes to him? What would we talk about? He was awfully cute, but still, I don't know. My mouth got ahead of my brain that time.

That night, Aunt Hannah came into my room. "Vicki," she said in her most actressy voice. "I can't have you staying in New York all summer and not seeing anything. This Sunday, I command you and your friend Stacey to join me for my superdeluxe tour of the city." I started to open my mouth and she raised her hand. "Nope, no objections. You don't have class and you have got to get out and have some fun. This Sunday, all right?"

"Aunt Hannah, all I was going to say was that would be great. Thanks."

She smiled, then looked at my blistered, Band-Aid–covered feet. "Good Lord, child. I look at your feet and suddenly the actor's life doesn't seem that hard anymore. We'll have fun Sunday. Don't stay up too late."

I turned off the light and lay down, looking out at the streetlight. I thought about Michael just for a second, but it made me feel too weird. I might kiss him—I know it wouldn't be like kissing Misha, but I need the practice. I've never kissed anybody. I think about it sometimes—what it would be like with Misha. I mean, I know what happens—my mom made sure of that. When I turned twelve, she sat me and Beth down with all her birth control equipment from the clinic and gave us a whole lecture. I was mortified and Beth kept laughing—she wanted to blow up the condom like a balloon. I got all the technical stuff. But that didn't explain the way I feel when I look at Misha in *The Turning Point* or in *White Nights*.

It didn't explain why my stomach flopped over when I was talking to Michael. That was the part that made me feel weird. I fell asleep thinking about Misha's hand on my face.

Sunday, Stacey showed up right at ten and we took off. First we went to the Empire State Building. It was jammed with people visiting from all over the world but we managed to fight our way to the edge of the balcony. The sun made everything flat and shiny and we were so high up that the wind rushed past our ears even though it was a hot day. We all looked over the edge and started laughing, even though nothing funny had happened. We were so far up that we couldn't even see individual people, just a flowing line of tiny cars. We tried to pick out Lincoln Center but we couldn't even find it among all the buildings. It was weird to have everything that seemed so important be so small all of a sudden. I thought of all the tourists that come here every day and look around and don't even know we're here. We're just part of the blur, just like everything was a blur to me as I looked down on the street.

On the way out, Stacey saw this guy who would take a penny and put it through this machine that flattened it out and pressed a picture of the Empire State Building onto it. Even though they were the same, Stacey and I each got one and traded. "That way, we'll always remember each other," Stacey said. We gave each other big, goofy grins.

"I want to take you guys downtown next," said Hannah in the elevator. "We should really check out SoHo."

"That's a weird name. Does it mean something?" asked Stacey.

"It's short for South of Houston Street. And if you want people to think you're from here, pronounce it HOWston, not HUston. That's the sure sign of a tourist. It's where there's a lot of art galleries," she said. Stacey and I made long faces. "And lots of cool stores," she added. We gave each other high fives. Aunt Hannah laughed. "Listen, we can go shopping first but there's one museum I really want to take you to. It's called the Museum for African Art."

The first place we went to was lower Broadway. There were hundreds of other kids there. Guys in big baggy pants and sweats, girls with big earrings, walking so close to each other it seemed they might start kissing at any minute. We went into a store where the music pounded so loud you could feel it in the soles of your feet, and a blond girl with black lipstick and a pierced nose tried on three different chokers before flinging them all back on the hanger in disgust and walking out.

Stacey and I laughed at her. She looked like nothing in any store, anywhere, would ever satisfy her. I got some cool earrings and Stacey got a really nice green miniskirt. Then we went to Tower Records and Stacey bought a CD and every other person seemed like they had somewhere to go, like they were going to be big record stars someday. Everything was important here. You could feel it.

Then we went over to Spring Street. People there were older but you could still feel the importance on your skin. Everybody looked like they'd stepped straight out of *Vogue* or *GQ*. They all seemed to be wearing black, even the ones that weren't. I looked around for Misha; it seemed like a cool enough neighborhood that we might run into him. But we didn't. We went to about a hundred stores but we didn't buy anything over there. We saw this one leather dress that was $200; it had straps all over it and pointed cones for your breasts and a kind of a dog collar attachment. Stacey and I both got the giggles just looking at it. Aunt Hannah tried to look serious but you could tell that she thought it was crazy too. It looked like something a kinky Barbie would wear.

After we got out of there, we went to the museum. I don't usually like art museums much but this was different. It was small, for one thing, and dimly lit. And the sculptures, from all over Africa, were amazing. It was like being in church. I remember when I was ten, my class came into the city to go the Metropolitan Museum and I saw a sculpture from Benin that looked just like my father. When I told him about it, he laughed and swung me up in his arms. He was so proud of me for seeing the resemblance. He said we all came from a long line of beautiful African people. He was always saying stuff like that. His eyes would shine and he would look so serious. He got mad at me later when I would start rolling my eyes and shifting from foot to foot when he talked about that stuff. But looking at these sculptures—I don't have the words for it—I understood what he was saying a little bit. Nothing could make the faces in those masks feel ashamed of who they were or what they looked like. My throat felt tight looking at them. They looked so strong. I tried to hang on to the feeling after we left the museum but it was hard. When I look at myself in the mirror or think about those girls on the subway, I don't see that same strength. I just see people. I don't see a whole history.

Stacey had gotten permission to stay over with me that night; I was glad. It was nice to share my room again with somebody even just for a night.

Even though Beth is a big pest, I'm used to having her to talk to and at least fight with. I'd never tell her, but I'd been missing her a little bit.

"So what did you think of the museum?" I asked Stacey as we got ready for bed.

"I liked it. It was so quiet. It made me think of Alvin Ailey in this weird way."

"What do you mean?" I said.

"Well, when I was little, they came to Chicago and my mom took me—I think it was the first dance performance I'd ever seen—and they did *Revelations*. It was amazing. It was like, I don't know, it was like being in a church and seeing what people went through in slavery and all that and still dancing, still doing stuff. Something about these sculptures reminded me of that. I don't know, maybe I'm not making sense." She stopped talking.

"No, I think I know what you mean. They made me feel like I was in church too. Different from ballet."

"Yeah." Stacey paused. "Sometimes I wonder if I want to keep doing ballet, you know? I see them looking at me funny because of the way I wear my hair and everything, but there's something about ballet, anyway. When it's going right I feel almost like I could fly, like there's nothing my body can't do. I don't know if I could get that somewhere else. But I know I stick out. And I know I always will in ballet. That's weird."

"Yeah. Well, at least we can stick out together," I finally said. She laughed.

We were both quiet for a minute, then I said, "You know that guy in Wendy's? He came up to me the other day and started talking to me."

"Ooooh, no he didn't. You're kidding."

"He did. He asked me if we could do something sometime. I said yeah."

"*Aaah!* No way!"

"Yes way. I feel kind of funny. I didn't really think I wanted to but he just kept standing there and next thing I know I was saying we should do something sometime when he asked."

"You know, Vick? I think you got potential, kid. Well, all I can say is you better keep me posted. I want *all* the gory details."

I threw a pillow at her. "Yeah, yeah. What makes you think there'll be any?"

"Mmm, I don't know. I just got a feeling."

I fell asleep thinking about what Stacey had said about us sticking out. I don't want to. I really want to be a part of all that perfection up there. If I work hard enough, I can be a part of it. Maybe then I won't stick out so much.

Chapter Five

After I said I would go out with Michael, I was sorry. I felt good at first; it was nice to have somebody ask me out and there was something very gentle in his eyes that I liked. But then all the voices crowded in: *He's not Misha. He works in a Wendy's. He might be one of those guys you see on the subway, acting so loud and ignorant.* What if we went out and he showed up wearing baggy jeans and was rude to Aunt Hannah? What if he tried to take me to some awful Arnold Schwarzenegger movie on Forty-second Street or something? I couldn't eat much, my stomach was too full of butterflies all the time. After a couple of days, Stacey finally asked me about it as we were getting ready for class. "So, what's up with that guy at Wendy's, what was his name, Michael?"

"I haven't been over there." I pretended to be

totally involved in wrapping my toes in lamb's wool. "Besides, you know how crazy it's been around here. I don't have time to mess with him."

Stacey regarded me coolly for a minute. "Well, I think you should make time, Miss Thing. If I didn't know better I'd say you were being a real snob. God, you could just see him on a Sunday or something. What's the big deal?"

I felt my face flush; it was like she'd seen into my head. "All right, all right. Let's go over there after class today." I scowled as I finished tying my shoes. Going to see Michael—it was like she was making me do it, even though it was something I told him I wanted to do.

I was able to forget about it during class; we were learning a new variation on pointe and that took up all my attention. I just about got it by the end of class, but my hair was frizzing out from the sides of my head and I could feel at least three new blisters starting. As soon as class was over, Stacey gave me a look and jerked her head toward the door. She wasn't going to let me off the hook.

After class, we went upstairs. These two girls in front of us were talking about the boys' classes—I just heard fragments.

"He's awfully cute."

"I don't know, though—I don't think you're his type, if you know what I mean."

59

"Oh man, him too?"

"Look, we don't do this stuff to meet guys. You know that."

A lot of girls—like these two—hang around the doorway and watch the boys and try to pick out who they want to partner with in adagio. They try to guess who's gay too—usually about half of the guys are—and then develop crushes on the rest. I've never done that. Stacey says none of the guys here interest her and Debbie had said at lunch (she'd already started taking adagio back home in Ann Arbor), "I'm trying not to even *look* at them this summer because I'm just gonna go home after and whichever one I like is probably gonna be gay anyway." I said that nobody had really grabbed me—which was true. But it was also true that I was looking for somebody like Misha, somebody magic. It didn't seem likely that Michael was going to fit that bill. That was another reason I didn't want to go over to Wendy's and finish what I'd started.

As we sat upstairs unwrapping our feet and talking, Debbie came up to us.

"What are you guys doing for lunch?" she asked. "Want to go get something?"

Stacey jumped in. "No, not today. Vick and I have a special errand to run. But maybe tomorrow?"

Debbie looked disappointed but then covered it with a smile and said, "Sure, okay. Tomorrow would be good."

"You know, Stace, I like Debbie but I get nervous talking to her," I said as we walked to Wendy's. "She's such a good dancer. Better than me."

Stacey gave me a funny look. "That may be," she said. "But you got the heart. Besides, she's really nice. And she's not stuck up at all. She's actually pretty cool for a white girl."

I took a deep breath. "Yeah? I don't know. I'm scared of her."

We were at the door of the restaurant now. "You, my dear," said Stacey, "are much too intense."

Stacey made me sit with her at a table right where Michael could see us, although we didn't order from him. He came up to us before we had even finished eating. "What's up, ladies?" he said.

"I'm doing fine," said Stacey, all bubbly.

"I'm okay." My voice sounded shaky.

"Cool. It's a beautiful day."

"Could you excuse me? I've got to run to the ladies' room," Stacey said. She wiggled her eyebrows at me as she left. Michael sat comfortably down in her chair. "So. I hope you meant it when you said we could hang sometime. I'd still like to."

"Yeah, I meant it." But my stomach was in knots.

"All right then. What are you doing this weekend?"

"Me, um, I have class on Saturday."

"Well, what about Sunday? I'm off that day."

"That . . . that would be okay, I guess. I'm staying with my aunt. She'll want to meet you." *And maybe she won't like your looks and I'll be saved after this,* I thought.

"That's cool. Listen, why don't you give me your number?" I looked away, frowning. He must have seen because he said, "I can give you my number if you want. But you have to promise we'll talk Saturday afternoon." He wrote his number neatly on the back of an order sheet.

Stacey was coming back from the bathroom. "Okay. I'll talk to you soon. I promise," I said. He smiled and the room suddenly seemed warmer. My stomach unknotted. "All right then. I'll see you," he said as he walked off.

Stacey sat down and leaned forward. "So? So? Spill, child."

"There's nothing to spill. I'm gonna see him on Sunday. Would you like to follow us?" I asked. I tried to make my voice mad but I was smiling a little.

"No, I would not like to follow you. I swear,

the way you act, girl, it's like you're being signed up for torture, not to spend an afternoon with a really cute guy."

It felt like torture. Not really. I mean, I kept telling him I wanted to go out with him and when he smiled, or looked at me a certain way, I really did want to see what he was like. I thought he might be fun. But then I'd get scared, thinking that he might not like any of the same things I like or that it might be awful or he might try to kiss me and have onion breath. Then I was scared and nervous. I didn't know how to explain that to Stacey. That's one of the best things about Misha. I know I wouldn't be nervous with him. At first maybe, but then he'd make everything all right. I can't count on Michael for that. I wasn't sure how to say any of that. So all I said was, "It's not torture. But I'm nervous. You know I never talk to any guys. I can barely get through an adagio class without freaking out."

"I know. But you gotta start somewhere. And he seems real nice. I'm jealous is what it is. You know how they keep us running from class to class so we hardly have time to think? I bet it's so we don't think about guys."

"You think so?"

"They wouldn't put it in so many words but that's what happens, isn't it?"

"Yeah. I guess. But if you're going to dance, it has to take up all your time. I mean, that's the only way to get any good at it."

Stacey scowled. "Maybe. Sometimes, though, I swear, I just want to bust out. I just get tired of doing what they say, when they say, all the time. I wish there was another way to dance."

Another way to dance. I never even think of another way; just getting to be the best I can at this way. I know about the girls who quit eating, taking class like so many skeletons; I know about Gelsey Kirkland, how crazy she went and how we never get to look at the world outside and how I probably can't go to college if I stick with it. But I don't care. This is all I can imagine doing. I don't think Stacey feels that way, hard as it is to understand. We are so different; what is it that keeps us together anyway?

One of the things I like best about Aunt Hannah is that she doesn't make such a big deal out of things. If I had told my mom about going out with Michael on Sunday, you would have thought I won the Nobel Prize or something. She would have been going on and on—"Oh, honey, I'm so excited for you, what are you going to wear, oh, I can't believe my little girl is growing up so fast."

But when I told Aunt Hannah, standing in the doorway of her bedroom, stubbing my toe on the floor, she just looked up from what she was reading and said, "That's great. I'd really like to meet him." Not another word about it, no big now-you're-a-woman talks or bear hugs or anything. Real calm, like this was no big deal. I couldn't help grinning at her. "Okay. He'll come by before we go out." I paused for a minute before I said, "You know, Aunt Hannah, you're really cool." She smiled back. "Thanks, Vicki. You're pretty cool yourself."

On Sunday afternoon, before Michael came over, I must have tried on four different outfits. I didn't know how I wanted to look. Older? Younger? Like I didn't care what he thought of me one way or the other? I finally ended up wearing jeans and a silk T-shirt Aunt Hannah lent me and my new earrings. I must have jumped ten feet in the air when the buzzer buzzed.

Waiting for him to come up in the elevator was the longest five minutes of my life. Hannah brushed at my shoulders to straighten the shirt out and said, "You look great," but I didn't believe her. She answered the door when the bell rang. I stayed in the living room but I heard her introduce herself and I heard his deep voice answering her. "Vicki," she called, "Michael's here!"

Michael was sitting on the couch with Aunt Hannah as I came out. He was wearing a denim shirt and black jeans that were a little big but not falling off his butt or anything. He didn't look like one of those loud homies on the train—I would have been nervous if he had. But he looked nice, really. Before we left, Hannah found out that he was sixteen, that he was in the tenth grade at Rice High School in Harlem, that he worked at Wendy's and that he planned to have me home by six-thirty. He kept taking tiny sips of the Coke that Aunt Hannah gave us—but he answered all her questions very fast and looked straight at her. She sat back as we got ready to leave with a look in her eyes that I knew meant she was pleased. "Listen, Michael," she said. "It was very nice to meet you. I didn't mean to rake you over the coals. But Vicki's mother would never forgive me if I didn't look out for her."

"Sure thing, Ms. Battle."

Aunt Hannah gave me a quick kiss. "Have fun, Vicki. I'll see you for dinner." And then we left.

In the elevator, Michael slumped against the wall. "Survived the third degree," he said, grinning and pretending to wipe sweat off his forehead. "Your aunt seems like a real nice lady, though."

"She's cool. I mean, I like her a lot," I answered.

I didn't know what else to say and it seemed like he didn't either. But then we both started to speak at once. "You first." "No, you first." This went on for a minute, then Michael finally laughed and said, "I just wanted to tell you that you look really nice."

My face got hot. "So do you. I like those pants. At least they stay up."

His eyes narrowed. "What do you mean?"

"I mean, you know, you see these guys on the street with their pants all hanging off them. You don't look like that." My voice got small in my throat as I talked.

"What does that mean?" he said. His voice climbed up a little, angry. "I'm black, just like them. So are you." He paused. "Or is that news to you?"

"No, it's not *news* to me." I was so mad I could feel my heart jammed up in my throat. But I was embarrassed too, like he'd caught me thinking something wrong, almost evil, somehow. "All I'm saying is that you look nice. I'm glad you aren't dressed like Ice Cube or something. My aunt wouldn't like it."

"And neither would you, huh?"

"No, I guess not." But I didn't feel mad anymore as he looked at me steadily, just ashamed.

Neither of us said anything for a while. Finally

67

Michael spoke. "I don't want this whole afternoon to get screwed up. I still want to get to know you better. But I gotta feel like I'm with somebody who isn't down on me—or herself. Is that you?"

"Yeah. I know what I sounded like. I'm not like that. I want to spend the afternoon with you too. Okay?"

"All right then. Let's go."

We walked for a while without talking. I was so nervous I could feel the top of my head prickling. "Where are we going anyway?" I said after we'd walked a little farther. "We've been walking for two blocks."

He looked up, his eyes still distant. I could feel my stomach start to ball up until he spoke. "I was thinking we could go over to Central Park," he said. "It's a nice day and . . . well, we don't have to do it if you think it's stupid . . . but they've got a zoo over there. It's hooked up. I like to go there on my days off."

I started smiling in spite of myself. "That would be great. Do they have seals?"

He started smiling too. "Yeah, you should see them. And the polar bears, when they're swimming around. I could watch them all day. The zoo's a ways down in the park but we could walk."

"Okay."

I noticed as we walked that he always made

sure that he was walking on the outside near the curb, even if he had to kind of run around me to do it. My mom told me once that used to be the polite thing to do but I'd never actually seen anyone do it. His mom must be real strict. "Have you always lived in New York?" I asked. It seemed like an old-ladyish question but I didn't know what else to say. I thought we should stick to a safe subject for a while.

"Yeah. Right up by a Hundred and Thirty-fifth since the day I was born. You been up there?"

"No. I've got so many classes and stuff I barely know my way around this neighborhood."

"I love it there. It's a mess but I love it. In the movies and stuff, they make it seem like it's all bad. Some of it's bad—the whole city's like that—but some of it's great too. When it's summer and brothers drive by with their windows open and the system boomin'. When you see a lot of little girls playing double Dutch in front of their stoop in the spring. The old houses. That part is cool. It's the other stuff that you gotta watch. The crackheads and the dope dealers. That's why my moms made sure that it's not all I know. That I know there's a world downtown too. Still, it's something. Maybe you could come up sometime; I could show you what it's really like. Am I making sense?"

"Yeah. I think I know what you mean."

"I love animals," he said. "Growing up here, it's not like I got to see them that much or anything but my moms took me to the zoo every chance she got. Every weekend, that was the only thing I wanted to do. I'd like to work in a zoo. Or be a vet maybe. Or a cowboy, take care of horses." He grinned. "I must sound crazy to you."

"No. No, you don't at all." I looked at him as we came to the entrance to the park. He looked like a million other guys. He could have been sitting with those girls on the subway, the ones who made me so nervous that time. But he had all this other stuff in his head. Just like I did. It made me like him even better—and it made me feel even worse about what I'd said before. I could hear my father's voice in my head—"Vicki, you know better than that. You know we all come from the same place." I spoke up, my voice small and shy. "Michael. What I said before, about your clothes and stuff. It was stupid. I'm really sorry."

He looked at me sharply. "That's all right. As long as you aren't all stuck up from living out in Jersey. Long as you know the real deal."

I hesitated, then spoke. "I think I do."

"All right then. How'd you start studying ballet anyway?"

"My mom took me when I was eight and I just went crazy. I thought it was the most perfect thing

I'd ever seen. Ever since then I've been taking classes. It's . . . I don't know. I just love it."

"You the only black person there?"

The back of my neck prickled. "There's one other one there. My friend that you met, Stacey. But I'm the only one at home in Jersey."

"That doesn't bother you?"

"You get used to it. Besides, I love ballet so much, I can't imagine not doing it." I paused. "There aren't that many black people working in zoos either, you know."

He grinned. "Ya got me. I know that. That's gonna be weird too. I'm not used to it, like you. And I don't know if I'll like it. But the animals, they don't care. They don't see me the way a lot of these people do. Maybe that's why I like them."

"Well, I don't see you that way," I said softly.

"I don't believe you do," he said as he pulled out his wallet. We were already at the entrance to the zoo. I hadn't even noticed how far we'd walked. "No, my treat," he said as I started fumbling around in my purse. "You can get it next time." Then he took my hand and led me through the gate.

He only held my hand for a minute. I was so surprised I couldn't even say anything. And I didn't mind—I liked it really. It made me feel breathless and light-headed for a minute—all I

71

could feel were the nerves in my hand under the warmth of his. Nothing was said but when he dropped my hand it seemed like things would be all right between us. We walked over to the seals without saying anything more.

The seal tank was beautiful. The seals darted around, smooth and bright gray, like they were flying. The water rippled around them; then they'd suddenly poke their heads out and bark at us. They looked awkward on their little island, shoving themselves around on their flippers. I liked it better when they were swimming. Michael laughed at everything they did; his eyes were big and shining just like all the little kids around us. We stood there for a long time before we went to the other exhibits.

It got easier and easier to talk as we walked around. About our families (he was an only child), about school (math and science were his favorite subjects; I hated both of them), about New York (he wished it was cleaner. So did I). We were standing in front of the polar bears, watching them lumber in and out of the water, when Michael said, "Hey, it's almost six. We gotta head back," looking at his watch. We headed out of the park and walked crosstown as the sun took on its sleepy late-afternoon orange.

Once we got home, Michael stood in front of

me, shifting from foot to foot for a minute. Finally, he said, "Listen, I meant what I said. I want to take you up where I live. Wanna do that sometime?"

"Well, like I told you, I'm taking ten ballet classes a week, but yeah, I would like to do that." I paused. "Maybe you could come to the ballet with me sometime too. We get cheap tickets 'cause of being students and all." I couldn't believe I said that so easily. He'd told me he'd never even been to a dance performance—why would he want to go to one now? My voice shook a little; I could feel the pressure in my throat. But once he smiled, I knew I'd done the right thing.

"Cool. That'd be really cool. All right then. I'll call you and we can figure out when you can come uptown with me. Okay?" I nodded and then he leaned over and kissed me, real quick, on the cheek and ran off.

I stood there rubbing my cheek like a little kid. For the first time in a long time, I wasn't thinking about Misha, I wasn't thinking about ballet. I wasn't thinking about what I did wrong with Michael or what I did right. I was just standing there, feeling the sun on my head. It was a nice feeling.

Chapter Six

Aunt Hannah was getting dinner out of the oven as I walked in. Jerk chicken and rice and peas—she used to date a guy from Jamaica who had his own restaurant. He taught her how to cook all kinds of Caribbean stuff. The house smelled of paprika and hot sauce, bright red smells. I was in such a good mood I was glad to smell it, even though it is really fattening. "Hey, you're home," she said as she straightened up from the stove. She looked at the clock. "And right on time too. What a polite boy." She grinned. "So how was it?"

Whenever we ate together, it was my job to set the table so I got plates and glasses down. "It was really fun, Aunt Hannah. I was so nervous at first but then we just started talking and he was just like anybody else."

"What'd you do? Where'd you go?" she said, setting down plates.

"We went to the zoo. It was really nice. He did the funniest thing too. He always walked on the outside of the sidewalk. Like if we got turned around and I was on the outside, he'd run around behind me so he'd be closer to the curb."

"Really? My God, I haven't seen a male—man or boy—do that in twenty years. Maybe longer. This boy's mama must not play around."

"Nope. I guess not."

I paused for a moment. "It started out kind of rough, though. I was trying to compliment him and he got mad."

Aunt Hannah looked at me. "What do you mean?"

"Well, I told him I was glad he wasn't dressed like those guys you see on the subway, you know, with their pants all hanging off and stuff. And he got mad. He said he was like them and so was I."

Aunt Hannah put down the saltshaker and turned to look at me seriously. "You know what he means, don't you?"

"I do." I sighed. "I mean, it's not like Dad didn't pound it into my head every day of my life. I know it's different for us, black people I mean. I didn't mean to make him mad. I just . . . I don't know. I was glad he wasn't wearing those pants. That's all I wanted to say. It turned out okay. I like him. And I think he likes me but it made me feel really weird. That's all."

Aunt Hannah looked at me for a long moment. I could tell she was thinking about what to say. Then she said, "As long as you guys talked it out. I trust you, Vicki. I don't want to give you a big lecture. I'm glad you had a nice time. Now let's eat."

I wouldn't have told my mom about that, or even admitted to her that I had a good time in spite of it. She just wouldn't have let it go. Aunt Hannah's easier to talk to somehow. We were almost like girlfriends, talking over dinner. She told me about her first date with a guy named Eric Kenyon, how he was so nervous when he came to pick her up that he called her mother Mr. Battle and her father Mrs. Battle. After that he was so embarrassed that he barely spoke except to apologize for the whole rest of the evening. "I kept telling him it was all right but there was no convincing him. Poor thing."

Just then, the phone rang. I ran to get it. It was my mom. "Hi, honey. How are you?"

"I'm good, Ma. Aunt Hannah and I were just finishing dinner."

"So everything's going okay?"

"Yeah. Class is going real well. We're going to find out soon who's going to be asked to come back for the fall and who isn't. I'm nervous about that."

"I bet. Well, I'm sure you'll be okay. Been doing anything else?"

"No." It was weird. I didn't want to tell her about Michael. I just didn't feel ready for the questions. I felt like she'd been waiting for this date or *some* date since I was ten and I wasn't even sure what I felt about him yet. I mean, I liked him, but somehow it was safer to keep it to myself for now. So I said, "Aunt Hannah took me and Stacey shopping in SoHo. I got some earrings. That was really fun. And we went up in the Empire State Building. That was cool too. So things are good."

"I'm glad, honey." She paused, not seeming to know what else to say. Finally, I broke into the silence. "You want me to get Aunt Hannah?"

"Yeah, thanks, honey. I'll talk to you soon."

I called Aunt Hannah and she came and took the phone. I went into my room and flopped on the bed. I thought about what I had said to Michael earlier about not looking like Ice Cube and how angry he had looked when he called me on it. I feel so confused sometimes. It's like I know what I mean—but I can't figure out how to tell it to anyone else. I'm not ashamed to be black—I don't think. I just wish it didn't matter so much. I really like Michael. I hope he knows that.

He said when we were looking at the polar bears that even though they were cooped up in this tank, you could see in their eyes how free they were. He hoped people could see that in his eyes, even when he was taking orders at Wendy's. He looked the way I imagined Misha would look when he talked about Leningrad, how beautiful it looked in the winter, with the snow falling everywhere and the old women making their way through the streets with scarves tied over their hair. I closed my eyes and saw him touching my cheek, gently, with a sad smile on his face. "It is so lovely there," he said, turning away from me and looking out his window at Central Park, spread out before him, the trees covered with snow. "I can never go back. I know that. I would miss my wine too much, the dancing here, everything. I don't miss fighting for every crumb I got. The KGB always knowing every step I took." He smiled. "But I wish you could see it. I wish you could hear the voices I grew up with. Sometimes, I still hear them in my head, even though I speak English all the time now. In my heart, I am speaking Russian still. Always." I came up behind him and put my arms around his waist. He turned away from the window. "But here I have you. Here, that is enough." Then he kissed me, his strong hands resting on the back of my neck.

Michael's kiss on the cheek was really nice but I couldn't imagine ever feeling the way I did about Misha about anyone else. The phone rang, startling me. I hadn't even heard Aunt Hannah hang up. "Vicki, it's Stacey calling," she yelled. I went and picked up the phone.

Stacey's voice, excited: "So? So? How was it? Are you gonna see him again? Did he try to kiss you?"

"Yeah, it was cool. He's nice. We went to the Central Park Zoo."

"The zoo? How corny! Did he buy you popcorn or something?"

"It wasn't corny! It was really nice," I said, more angrily than I meant to. "Besides, what brilliant idea do you think he should have come up with?"

Stacey's voice dropped, like a little kid who's been scolded. "I don't know. Something more glamorous, I guess. I just thought—"

"God, I mean you're talking like he's Mr. Smooth or something. He's just a guy who works in Wendy's. And it was the first time I've ever been out with a guy. It was nice. My aunt wouldn't let me run the streets at night with a strange boy anyway. Honestly, Stacey. You're so harsh sometimes."

"Dag. Sorry. I guess you do like him."

I still felt mad for him. "Yeah," I said. "I guess I do."

"Well, I don't know, Vick. You just seemed so hesitant before you guys went out and stuff. It was like you didn't think you'd have a good time at all. I thought you'd hate going to the zoo."

I sighed. "You're right, I guess. I was acting like that. But I don't feel that way anymore. I had a really good time. He's nice."

"And cute," Stacey said. "Did he try to kiss you?"

"Just on the cheek."

"Dag. A real gentleman and all. I'm sorry I said what I said before, Vick. Sounds like he might be a winner."

"Yeah," I said. "He just might."

Chapter Seven

After we went out, I didn't hear from Michael for a couple of days. I thought he might still be mad about what I had said when we first got together. He'd seemed happy and like he meant it when he said he wanted to take me uptown but then the phone didn't ring and didn't ring and I was just beginning to think I'd imagined the whole thing and that my first date was going to be my last when, one night, the phone finally rang.

"Hey, it's Michael. What's up?"

"Michael. Hi. I was starting to wonder if I was going to hear from you."

"Look, don't be all mad. It's only been a couple of days. I was hoping that you would call me. You could have, you know."

Busted. He was right, of course. I could have called him instead of waiting around to hear from him. "You're right. I guess I just felt . . . I don't know . . . I wanted to hear from you first."

We were both quiet for a minute. Then he said, "Well, I'm glad. I've been thinking about you. I've just been busy." I could hear the smile in his voice.

"So," I said, smiling myself, "when do you want to show me around Harlem?"

"How about Sunday?"

"I've gotta check with my aunt but that should be okay."

"Cool. I'll come pick you up around—ten."

"Ten in the morning?"

"Yeah. I got something special I want to do."

He made me curious. But after we talked, I didn't think about it much the rest of the week. We were working on some new steps in pointe class and a very difficult variation in adagio class and that started to take up a lot of space in my head. Josh was really nice about it but I was having a terrible time getting my weight balanced so he could lift me right. We stayed after class every day all week working on it. "You know," he said finally, after the tenth time trying and failing to do the lift, "you've really got to relax in order to do this. Be there, but let me do it. It feels like you're fighting me the whole time."

I sighed. "Okay, okay. Let me just have a minute." I went to the corner and had a drink of water from the bottle I carry. I shook my hands at my sides. I tried to let my mind be empty. Nothing there, just my legs and arms and hands moving. I turned back to Josh. He counted out loud. We did the lift. I was flying and then I landed. Light. On my toes quick and light. Josh was grinning. "Now you got it. That was great."

We stood there smiling at each other for a minute. Those are the best parts of ballet. The parts worth doing it for. But they don't come much. This summer, I'd noticed that even when they did come, I didn't look like some of these other girls here. I looked okay—I'm a pretty good dancer— but something was missing. Whatever it was that somebody like Misha had—or even some of the girls in the corps—I didn't have it.

"Was it really great, Josh? Really?"

"Yeah, you're a good dancer."

The words came out before I had a chance to think about them. "How good?"

Josh looked like he'd just swallowed a frog. "How good?"

"Yeah. Good enough to come back in the fall, you think?"

"Um, I don't know. I like dancing with you. I think you're good. But you know how hard it is to get asked back. I don't know. I don't even know if I'm going to get asked back." He paused. "Why'd you ask me that?"

"I'm sorry. I didn't mean to put you on the spot. It's just . . . I don't know. It's so hard to know if you're good enough and nobody can tell you. I don't know why I asked you. It just felt good to get that combination right."

He looked at me thoughtfully but didn't say anything for a minute. "I hope that you do come back," he finally said.

"Thanks. I hope you do too. I'll see you tomorrow."

"Yeah."

I don't know if I'm going to be asked back. But I think Josh was telling the truth. I've gotten better this summer but I don't move the way Debbie does or some of the girls who are already in the corps. I feel a little scared when I think about it. In moments like with Josh, when it feels right and I'm really dancing, I can't believe I might not get asked back. But other times, I think I'm good but not good enough. I went into the bathroom for a minute and went into one of the stalls. I sat down on the toilet and pulled out my *Vanity Fair* with Misha on the cover. I took a deep breath and stared into his eyes for a long time. My mind was blank.

Aunt Hannah said it was okay for me to go out with Michael on Sunday so he was at our house early. He'd told me to dress up, so I did, wearing a skirt and a little bit of Aunt Hannah's lipstick (she swore she wouldn't tell my mother. I'm not supposed to wear makeup until I'm sixteen). Michael was all dressed up too, in a jacket and tie. Aunt Hannah said as she opened the door, "My goodness, don't you look nice. Where are you off to?"

Michael looked a little sheepish. "Church first. My mom and I go to Abyssinian uptown. Then I was just going to show Vicki around my neighborhood."

I don't know if my face showed anything. But in my head I was like, "Church? Really?" My parents don't go anymore. We went when I was little but I don't really remember much about it. It was Episcopalian, I think. I remember always wishing it was over. And I remember drawing pictures in Sunday school. That's about it. And now Michael was taking me there, with his mother, for a date. Aunt Hannah had a funny look on her face too. Not bad, just a little surprised. "Well," she finally said. "You guys have a good time. Vicki, I'll see you at four." Then we left.

On the way down in the elevator, Michael said, "You don't mind, do you? My mom wanted to meet you and I go with her every Sunday. We won't be there all day, though. Is that okay?"

"Yeah, sure." The way he was looking at me, I felt like I'd be the worst person in the world if I didn't say it was okay to go. I didn't say anything for a minute, then I finally said, "Do you like going?"

"It's okay. A lot of guys I hang out with think it's stupid. Sometimes it is kind of boring, but sometimes I like it. I don't know. My moms says I'll appreciate it when I get older."

"Moms are always saying that stuff, aren't they?"

He laughed. "You know it."

On the subway, it was weird. After Ninety-sixth Street going uptown, there are hardly any white people on the train anymore. It's like there's some rule that they all have to get off there. I said something to Michael about it and he laughed but he looked a little angry too. "Yeah, it's the great divide," he said.

We kept going all the way up to 135th Street, talking the whole way about school and stuff. The church was just a few blocks away from there. There were open hydrants with kids darting through the spray and guys in kente cloth hats selling T-shirts and little African-looking sculptures. Broken glass sparkled in places on the street, glittering and sharp-looking. The church was off Broadway on 138th Street but I knew we were coming up on it about a block ahead. We kept seeing more and more little girls in ruffly, new-looking dresses and women in amazing hats with veils and feathers and all kinds of stuff. I started to feel really underdressed. As we walked up the street, a beautiful, tall woman with long dreads and dark skin walked toward us. "Michael. Hi, honey. I was starting to worry. You must be Vicki. I'm Sarah Bowman. Call me Sarah." She said all this very fast and stuck her hand out for me to shake while she was talking and turning toward the church to go in. I took her hand quickly and said, "Nice to meet you . . . Sarah."

We went into the church and found a pew near the front. Michael's mom seemed to know everybody that came in, practically. And they all stopped and said something to Michael too. Everyone seemed to have known him since he was a little boy. There were hardly any other guys Michael's age there.

Once the service started, I gradually stopped feeling so weird. The sermon was long. The only part I remember was the minister talking about how important it was to stand up for yourself and not let anybody make you feel ashamed. He said that's how God would want it. But then the singing started. It was like an electric charge went through the whole church as the choir shuffled to its feet, royal blue robes swinging. When the soloist opened her mouth and started singing, the back of my neck started tingling. Like the first time I saw Misha in *The Turning Point*. I knew I was hearing something perfect. Her voice sounded like it could make the whole church explode if she wanted it to. Like she could rise up and fly if she just tried hard enough. The choir members behind her rocked and swayed, their robes moving in the light. Heads bobbed and feet shuffled behind me and people who knew the words joined in. It made my head feel buzzy, like my heart had left my body and gone to the stage where the singers were.

After the service, Mrs. Bowman, I mean Sarah, and Michael and I stood out on the church steps. Kids chased each other back and forth as their mothers yelled over their shoulders for them to cut it out, they were gonna get all messed up. Sarah looked at me hard for a minute. Her eyes looked like lights on a very dark road. "So, did you enjoy the service, Vicki?"

"Yes, I did. It was really great."

"Mmm. Well. This is one of the best. Been coming since I was a little girl. Michael tells me you're a dancer."

"Yes, I study ballet at School of American Ballet."

"I used to study dance. Not ballet, though. I studied with Martha Graham. My goodness, that was something." She looked off into the distance for a minute. "Well, I hope that you persist, wherever it may lead for you. It's an extraordinary way to spend your life, dancing. There's always music in your head."

I didn't know what to say so I just smiled. She went on. "I suppose you kids have plans. That's fine. Michael, I'll expect you home by four-thirty. You have a lot of homework to do."

"Yeah, Moms. I'll be there. See ya."

She offered her cheek for a kiss and Michael kissed her, quick, like he didn't want anybody to catch him doing it. As we headed down the steps, he grabbed my hand.

"So," he said. "What did you think?"

"Of church?" I said. "It made me feel like the top of my head was going to come off. It was amazing. Your mom's beautiful. I never would have thought of doing this but it was really fun."

"Yeah. Well, I thought you might like it. I don't know why. There aren't too many people I'd bring up here for this. Not even that many of my buds know I go."

"Really?"

"Yeah. Church with your moms? That's *too* funny."

We walked along without talking for a while. Then I finally said, "You never told me your mom was a dancer."

"Yeah. She never talks about it. She dropped out sometime in the sixties, when she started hanging with my father. She never took me to any dance or anything."

"It'll be fun when we go then. I mean, if you still want to."

He looked at me for a minute. "I do."

We'd been walking this whole time but I hadn't even been paying attention. "Where are we going?"

"You'll see."

Finally we stopped in front of this little restaurant called Johnny's Chicken & Ribs. It looked *gr-eeesy*. Michael laughed as we went in. "You are now about to enter the home of the best fried chicken in New York," he said.

Fried chicken? Oh my God. How was I going to eat even one mouthful without gaining eight million pounds? And how was I going to tell Michael that I couldn't eat here? I followed him through the door looking at the backs of his shoes.

Inside, it smelled spicy and warm. The outside was grubby-looking but inside was really clean. The tables were covered with plastic flowered tablecloths and people were everywhere, leaned over plates piled with food, some with napkins tucked into their shirtfronts to avoid messing up their clothes. A lot of people were wearing just-came-from-church outfits and everyone was talking and laughing.

Michael eased us into a small table in the corner and the waitress brought us menus. Fried everything. It did smell good but . . . I just couldn't. "I'll have the side salad, please," I said. "And a diet Coke."

"And I'll have the fried chicken and greens. And a root beer," said Michael. He turned to me and said, "You don't look like you need to be on any kind of diet."

"I'm not on a diet exactly. I just have to be careful what I eat. You know how skinny the girls in my school are. I have to stay that way too."

"Mmm. Well. I wouldn't do it. And miss out on some Johnny's? No way."

When they brought his food, it did look good. My salad was okay but it was seeming a little thin. Everyone else seemed to be enjoying whatever they were eating a lot more. Usually, I can just think about school and resist temptation, but I don't know, something about the singing in church or something, I found myself saying to Michael, "Can I get a piece of your chicken? I changed my mind."

"Sure. I was gonna ask you again." He speared me a drumstick. I ate it. He was right. It was the best fried chicken I'd ever had. I wanted to ask for some more but I didn't dare. I had class tomorrow.

"Now see what you would have missed if you hadn't asked me for a little bit of that?" he said.

"Yeah. Yeah, I do." I swear, I do more things I never thought I would do when I'm with him.

We talked a lot while we ate. Michael told me all about his mom, how she used to be in the Black Panthers (so was his dad. That's how they met and that's why she quit dancing) but then everything got crazy and she got pregnant and had to get a paying job and decided to finish school. She finished college and Michael started kindergarten the same year.

"She never talked to you about dancing?" I asked when he was done.

"Nope. Hardly at all. That thing she just said to you—I didn't know she felt that way about it. But that's how my moms is. When something's over, it's over. Time for the next thing."

92

"So she left it just like that?"

"Like I said, she never talked to me about it, but yeah, it must have been something like that."

"Wow. I don't know what I'd do if I stopped dancing."

"Well, like my moms. She's a lawyer now. She helps people that can't afford a lawyer on their own. But she didn't start doing that till I was already in second grade. It took her a while to figure it out. She's happy now, though. I know she loves her job. So I guess you can change. If you want."

Change if you want. The words stuck in my head but I wasn't sure why. It just stayed there—the thought that wanting something might not be enough to get it, that you might have to change anyway.

"My mom's a great lawyer too," he finished proudly. "That's what I want to be, when I start being a vet. The best."

"Yeah, me too, when I start dancing full-time." We just sat there grinning at each other like a couple of fools. "Come on," Michael said. "We've got a lot to see today."

We went everywhere. To the open-air market on 125th, full of kente cloth hats and bootleg videos—I swear, they had movies up there that hadn't even shown up in theaters yet. We went to a pickup basketball game on an open-air court and joined in the yelling, cheering crowd for a little while. We went to this place called Aunt Len's Doll Museum, which was this woman's house who was just crazy about dolls—she had thousands of them in every available space. It was incredible. It was like my wildest dream when I was about eight but now it seemed kind of creepy. My eyes felt full of lace dust when we left there. We went past some really beautiful places but there was always sadness around the next corner too—once we saw this brownstone where every window had a flower box in the middle of a block where every other building had boarded-up windows.

Finally, we ended up at this playground with benches, just to rest a minute before I headed home. There were little kids everywhere, swinging and running around but a lot of the equipment was missing and what was there was beat up. But the kids seemed to be having fun anyway. "You see why I like it here and then I don't," said Michael. "It's like it's two places, beautiful and not beautiful and the two keep bumping up against each other all the time. I think I'll always want to live here—or someplace like it. But in some ways I just want to run and run and run. You know what I'm saying?"

"Yeah, I think I do." We both looked down at some little girls playing double Dutch and laughing. They didn't pay any attention to us at all.

Chapter Eight

We had open class about a week after that and my mom and Beth came up to visit. The two of them and Aunt Hannah came to watch class. It was an okay class, not a great one, but the way they carried on after, you'd think I was already starring in *Swan Lake* or something. All the "Oh, Vicki, you were so marvelous," and "You've really gotten so good this summer." It's nice that they were so impressed, but I knew that my pirouettes weren't stable enough and I needed to get my leg higher in arabesque.

We all had dinner together that night. Even picking the restaurant was an adventure. Beth started in as soon as we got home. "Ma, let's go to Planet Hollywood! I saw on *Entertainment Tonight* that Arnold Schwarzenegger owns it and Bruce Willis and maybe there'll be some movie stars there or something. Let's go there."

"Aww, Ma. That place is so tacky. No movie star would be caught dead in there. All it is is all these tourists from God knows where. Aunt Hannah told me. And it's all hamburgers and stuff. I can't eat there," I said.

Ma gave Aunt Hannah an exasperated look. "No movie stars, Hannah? Are you sure?"

"They don't eat there, but you guys might find it fun. It has all this stuff on the walls that different actors have donated. You don't get to the city that much and Vicki, you're here for three more weeks. Maybe we should go where Beth wants this time."

"Aunt Hannah, I *know* that, but Planet Hollywood? Come on!"

"I agree with Hannah," my mom said. "You and I can go wherever you want for lunch tomorrow but tonight . . . it's Planet Hollywood."

Beth started screaming like a banshee and ran to *my* room to change. I threw my mom and Hannah a dirty look and went after her. "And no attitude, young lady," my mom shouted after me.

Beth was rummaging through her suitcase but she stopped when she saw me come in. "Oh come

on, Vick. It'll be fun. Maybe they'll have somebody's old ballet shoes there."

"Very funny. We always get to do what you
want."

"Oh, right. Listen, Vick. I'm not the one who
gets to stay in New York all summer, running all
over town, doing whatever she wants. I'm not the
one who Mom's always telling her friends about.
I'm not the one who everybody thinks is so great."
She sat back on the bed, her lip pushed out.

"Come on, Beth. You really mean that? Everybody thinks I'm so great?"

"You're all Mom ever talks about at home. I
might as well be invisible."

I just looked at her. "Well, compared to most
of the girls up here, I'm nothing to write home
about," I finally said.

Beth just grunted. I didn't know how to con-
vince her that I really didn't want to be treated any
different. I didn't feel like such a winner myself
after most classes. But I didn't know how to tell
her.

When my dad left, Beth and I were each
other's best friends for a while. Even though lots of
people's parents were divorced it seemed so horrible that we couldn't tell anybody else about it. We
walked to school together every day and would sit
in my room every night I didn't have class, look-

ing at magazines, talking a little, wondering if he'd come back. I knew we were getting used to my parents being separated when we had our first fight after he left. Beth had borrowed my favorite skirt and gotten ink on it. I was like, "Ma, I'm gonna kill her."

"I told her I was sorry. I can't help it. My pen top fell off and I didn't even know it."

"Sorry. If you wouldn't take my stuff without asking, you wouldn't be messing it up all the time."

My mom just stood looking at us. "Girls, I want both of you to stop this nonsense right now. Beth, you know you're not supposed to take Vicki's things. And Vicki, I think we can get that stain out at the dry cleaner's. Now I want both of you to go to your rooms to cool off."

We did. And everything cooled off. We stopped walking to school together every day, and things went back to the way they had been. Sometimes we were buddies but mostly we weren't. I never asked her, but I think that's when we both stopped believing that Dad was ever going to come back. There was nothing said. We just knew.

Looking at her pouting out the window, I felt some of the way we'd felt when he first left: some of that same closeness. But I didn't know how to say it. So I sat down next to her on the bed so that our legs almost touched. She didn't move away. We both jumped a little when Ma called us to hurry up and get ready to go.

We took a cab over to the restaurant. It was packed—and just like I said, there were a ton of tourists. Aunt Hannah shot me a conspiratorial look over Beth's head. But once we got seated, I have to admit, it was kind of fun. No ballet shoes, but it was kind of neat looking at all the other autographed stuff they had. I thought Beth was gonna bust she was so excited. She especially liked Patrick Swayze's jacket from *Dirty Dancing*. She made us all come look at it. My mom and Hannah acted like they were impressed but I'm not sure they really were. I saw them giving each other a look.

Once we were all eating (they did have some salads so it was okay; I'd already fallen off the wagon once this week) and had finished exclaiming over Patrick Swayze, Hannah looked cautiously at my mother and said, "So I talked to Jason a little when he was up here. It seems like he's doing okay." Jason is my father. He and my mom and Hannah all went to Howard University together. Beth and I both looked up, still as statues in a museum. Ma's face looked like a door had closed in it. I suddenly thought of the last big fight

Ma and Dad had, the one before she asked him to leave. They were right in the living room. They didn't even try to hide. My dad started it—he was complaining about the house always being a mess with my dance stuff and little parts from motors that Beth was taking apart lying around. I heard the whole thing from my bedroom.

"Jason, I just cannot take any more of this. Nothing ever satisfies you. I can't stand it."

"Damn, Alicia. It's not like I ask for that much. Just for the house to be halfway decent and for you to act like you halfway care whether I still live here."

"Yeah, well, sometimes I wonder."

Dad was quiet for a long time. I imagined the stunned look on his face. "Well, if you find yourself wondering, I find myself wondering if I need to stay. I'm not so sure."

"I'm not so sure either." I could hear her footsteps walking quickly out of the room. He left a week later.

I felt like I was going to cry, remembering. I had to swallow a lot of times right there in the middle of the restaurant. Then I heard Ma's voice out of the din all around us. "I'm glad to hear that, Hannah. You know I wish him the best," she said, her voice icy cool. Hannah looked like she

101

wished she hadn't said anything. "Hey, did I ever tell you guys about the time I worked with Kevin Costner?"

"Oooh, no, Aunt Hannah. What's he look like in person?" Beth said, all excited, like she wanted to change the subject.

"The man is finer than frog's hair. And nice? Well, this was a long time ago, just in a commercial, before he was a big star. But he was one of the nicest guys I ever worked with." She was off and running. But I only half listened. I kept looking at my mother like a stranger. She just kept eating, laughing at the funny parts of Aunt Hannah's story like nothing had happened.

I rubbed the bridge of my nose. It made me mad, the coolness in her voice when she talked about my father, like she'd never loved him at all. I don't see how that can change so quickly. I feel like I'm going to love Misha forever, like it's a permanent part of me. Did Ma ever feel that way about Dad? And if she did, how could it end? What did she do with all that feeling? I just don't get it.

When I tuned back in to the conversation, Aunt Hannah was talking to my mom. "So, Alicia, what do you think of Vicki's big dates, huh? Two of them now."

My mom looked startled. "Dates? What dates?"

I felt sick. I hadn't told her. I had talked to her a couple of times since Michael and I went out but every time I thought of telling her I'd imagine the shrieks and the questions and I just didn't want to deal with it. Somehow it didn't bother me as much when Aunt Hannah asked things or when Stacey did, but with my mom it was like I'd won some kind of prize she never thought I'd get. It just bugged me. But now she was looking at me, her eyes wide, and I wanted to drop through the floor.

"Vicki, you've been dating someone?"

I sighed. "Yeah. I mean no. I mean, we just went out a couple of times. It's no big deal."

Beth started singsonging, "Vicki's got a boyfriend, Vicki's got a boyfriend," until Aunt Hannah shushed her. My mom went on. "Where'd you meet this boy?"

"At the Wendy's where I eat a lot. It's no big deal, Ma. Aunt Hannah met him and she liked him and I'm sorry I didn't tell you. I was going to." That last wasn't totally a lie. I would have had to tell her eventually. Just like I was doing now.

She sat back with a sigh. "Well. I don't want to get into this now, Vicki, but I sure wish you'd told me. I think it's wonderful that you're making some new friends and dating a little bit. You know I always worried about that."

"Yeah, Ma. I know." *And that's why I didn't tell you,* I thought. I was tired of being worried over. Ma acted like I was special, I guess, but not the way I wanted. It was like everything I did right was some kind of shock to her. I never felt that way with Aunt Hannah. And I knew I wouldn't feel that way with Misha. He'd expect nothing less of me. We finished dinner without saying any more about it. But I knew we'd be getting back to it soon.

Chapter Nine

The next day, my mom let me pick a restaurant like she'd promised and just the two of us went out for lunch. I was dreading it. She hadn't said any more about Michael last night but I kept catching her looking at me, pressing her hand to her mouth the way she does when she's upset about something. I wished I'd just told her about him. But it was too late now. I picked this place on Columbus Avenue that Misha owns. I ordered a salad and a diet Coke, just like I always do.

"Do you ever eat anything else, hon?" Ma asked.

"Yeah, sure I do. Don't worry, Ma. Aunt Hannah already gave me the big I-gotta-eat lecture. Look at me—do I look anorexic?"

She smiled. "You look beautiful, honey. But

you know I worry. I know how many girls stop eating when they get really serious about dancing. Remember when they had to take that girl out of your school?"

"I remember." Her name was Suzanne. She was a really good dancer but at least once a week after class, if you went in the bathroom at the wrong time, you could hear her throwing up in one of the stalls. She must have been doing it every day at home. But none of us ever said anything. She was so skinny and that's what they kept telling us we should be. But I'm nowhere near like she was. I can't believe that my mom thought I might be. "I'm just careful about what I eat, Ma, that's all. Don't get all freaked out, okay?"

"I am not freaked out," she said, her voice precise and strained. "I'm just concerned about you. I haven't seen you in two weeks." She paused. "And you've changed so much in that little bit of time. I just worry about you. That's all."

"Well, you don't have to."

She pressed her lips together. I could almost hear her trying not to get mad at me. But I didn't care. My throat felt tight, but I didn't care. "Remember when I took you and Beth both to see *The Nutcracker* that first time?" she said.

"Yeah." It was cold and we were all dressed up. I was wearing this blue polka-dot dress with all this stiff lace under the skirt. It was itchy but I loved the way it would swirl as I spun around, the lace peeking out. When we were sitting there and the "Dance of the Snowflakes" came on and all that snow started floating down—I stopped breathing. It was magic. And there were all these little kids—the same age as me—right in the middle of it. I drove Ma crazy for the next month begging for lessons. Beth didn't even seem to care what we'd just seen. She said she thought it was boring. But she's crazy.

Finally, my mom came home one day with a big bag that she kept behind her as she came into my room while I was doing my homework. I was listening to the *Nutcracker* music on my tape player. "Guess what I have in this bag, Vicki," she said. She was smiling. She looked so beautiful. I said I didn't know and then she reached in and pulled out pink tights and a black leotard and pink ballet shoes. "I've signed you up at a school downtown. I figured anything you could stick to asking me for the way you've stuck to this, you must really want. You start Monday."

I jumped out of the chair, knocking it over and hugged her around the waist as tight as I could, screaming my head off. I could smell the musky Halston perfume she always wore. My dad stood in the doorway, grinning. It was the happiest I've ever been. Now sometimes it seems like a dream I had once. Except that I'm still dancing. That's how I know it was real.

I didn't say anything, though. Just repeated, "Yeah, I remember."

"I'm glad that you've stuck with this, honey," she said. "I know it doesn't always seem like I'm glad, but when I saw you in class yesterday, I knew you were doing something you loved. It's hard for me to understand—it seems so difficult and so isolating—but you're really good at it. I'm very proud of you."

If she really saw me, she'd see how much better somebody like Debbie is than me. But she doesn't, and I didn't want to try to make her see. So I just said, "Thanks," and fiddled with my Coke straw.

We sat in silence for a few minutes. She looked tired to me—there were big circles under her eyes. But she kept smiling at me like she hoped I'd jump up and throw my arms around her or something. I remember wanting to do that—sometimes, when I'm scared, I still want to—but I don't anymore. She ruined everything. Her and my stupid father too, I guess, but mostly her. I can't forget that. Finally, she spoke. "You know what I want to ask you, don't you?"

"I have a pretty good idea."

"Vicki, why didn't you just tell me about this

boy—his name's Michael, right? You know that I'm really happy for you."

"I don't know, Ma. I just didn't think of it."

"Do you really expect me to believe that?"

I sighed. "No. I guess not. I really . . . I just didn't want you to make a huge deal out of it. I've only been out with him twice and I just didn't want it to be such a big thing."

She stirred her iced tea thoughtfully. "You think I make too big of a deal out of everything, don't you?"

My eyes filled with tears. I felt totally stupid. "Yeah, yeah I do. I just don't like being fussed over so much, that's all. It makes me feel weird."

I could feel her looking at me steadily. "Ever since you were little, you've put so much pressure on yourself, hon," she finally said. "I remember when you were just six and you came home so upset because you couldn't write cursive like the other kids. I heard a noise and came in your room at one in the morning and there you were, up with a flashlight under the covers, writing those Palmer method curves over and over." She swallowed hard. "I said to myself then that I'd always be sure to praise you and make you see just how special you are. Just you. Without having to lay all those trips on yourself. But I don't know if it's working."

I didn't know what to say. I was afraid if I spoke I'd start crying. Everything was such a mess.

"I'm sorry that your father and I have made things so hard for you. But we had to do it. We couldn't live together anymore. I just couldn't stay married like that anymore. You see, don't you?"

I didn't see. I didn't see at all. But I couldn't say that to her. The look on her face—it was like she was going to start bawling any minute. Her voice was small and strained as she talked. I wiped my eyes with the back of my hand quickly. "I'm sorry, Ma. It just makes me feel really bad."

She reached across the table and took my hand. "I know. It makes me feel really bad too."

She let go of my hand and we ate silently for a while. Finally she took a deep breath and said in a brighter voice, "So are you enjoying your classes? How's it going?"

"Good. I've been picked to demonstrate a couple of times."

"Is that good?"

"Yeah, Ma." I felt a little exasperated. "It's really good. Everybody wants to get picked to demonstrate."

"Well, good for you, hon. Are you making friends?"

"I told you about Stacey, right? She's great. But

110

she's the only one so far. It's hard. Everybody's kind of competing against each other."

"That must be hard."

"Yeah. I'm hanging in, but that part is hard."

I hadn't thought about that thing with me writing cursive for a long time. I remember her coming into the room, softly, smelling like sleep and sweat and pulling the blanket off my head. She took the flashlight away from me very gently and sat down on the edge of the bed. I remember her hand stroking my head and the sound of her singing. I didn't even hear her leave the room— she stayed until I was sound asleep. I wish I could tell her everything, about Michael and Misha and how mad I am at her and Dad for breaking up but I just couldn't. All the words stuck in my throat. I couldn't get them out. I just smiled a little and said, "I'm doing okay, Ma. Don't worry about me."

We finished lunch and I talked a lot as we walked home, showing off like I lived in the city all the time or something. I pointed out where John Lennon used to live. But I think we both felt sad. Beth was all packed when we got home and my mom went into Hannah's room to talk to her before they left. I punched Beth in the arm. "So you guys are heading back now?"

"Yeah." She paused. "So you'll be home in three weeks, huh?"

"Yep. Why?"

She looked embarrassed. "I miss you."

I was surprised but wanted to give her something back. "I miss you too, peanut-head. But I'll be home soon. We'll get sick of each other in nothing flat."

She grinned. "Yeah, I guess so. Can I borrow your black jacket before you come home?"

I sighed. "I guess so. But if you spill anything on it, you're dead."

Beth was nodding and laughing and pretending to kiss my hand when Ma came out with her overnight bag. "Well, Beth, I guess we're off." She hugged Aunt Hannah quickly. "I'll talk to you soon, girl." Then she gave me a big long hug. "Remember what I said, Vicki. I'm here if you want me. I only want you to let me in, okay?"

"Yes, Ma."

"I love you very much, hon."

"I love you too, Ma."

I waved from the street in front of Aunt Hannah's as they drove away. I felt a lot older than I had been three weeks ago when they brought me up here.

Chapter Ten

Some days, you get out of bed and have a bad feeling from the second you open your eyes. You look at the ceiling and it seems lower, like everything's pressing in on you. The rooms get smaller as you walk around. That's what this day was like. Even with Aunt Hannah. We usually get along great, but today she was getting on my nerves *bad*. It started at breakfast. I was only having juice and Aunt Hannah gave me a real serious look. "Vicki, I'm a little worried about you. I told your mama I'd look out for you and the fact is, I've scarcely laid eyes on you since we went to SoHo a couple of weeks ago. And when you are here, you hardly eat a thing."

"Oh, Aunt Hannah, I'm all right. I always eat lunch, yogurt or something, at school. Breakfast makes me sick."

"Well, sick or not, you need to eat. You're spending so much energy at school. It's important."

"Okay. Okay." I got a box of cereal down, poured some, and ate it noisily. "How's that?"

"That's better. Look, baby," she said, her eyes softening. "I'm your mother's closest friend. And I don't want this to turn into a war between us. We've always been buddies, right?"

"Right." I could feel the cereal congealing in my stomach.

"And I want us to stay that way. I know how hard dancing is. Really. And I think I know how much it means to you. But I've got to look out for you. Please let me."

"Okay."

She kissed me on top of my head. "I've got to run to an audition. You have a good day now, you hear?" I stuck my tongue out at the door as it slammed behind her.

It's weird about food. I know I'm not anorexic. Even though Aunt Hannah's all worried, I eat too much to be. And the thought of making myself barf all the time is just too gross. But I do have to be real careful what I eat. We just talk about it so much in the dressing room and stuff and everybody looks at you funny if you confess to having anything but lettuce and yogurt at meals. Like that

114

little bit of fried chicken I had with Michael. I would never have told anybody about that, not even Stacey. I guess some people would think it's weird but it feels good in a way. I actually feel sort of clear and pure when I don't eat much, like I'm better somehow, a better dancer or a better person. I know how bad it can get and I know I'm not there. But I still wish she hadn't made me eat breakfast. It made me feel gross.

Then in class, I was klutz of the century. I could not do anything right. Turned the wrong way when we did pirouettes, couldn't get my arabesque to stick, nothing. Every movement was like a stick figure. Finally, at the end, we all had to do *tours jetés* across the floor and as I landed from mine I lost my balance and fell flat on my butt. Oh my God.

Miss Reinman and everybody came over and I jumped up right away, my face hot. "I'm fine, I'm fine, really."

"Everybody falls at some point, Vicki," said Miss Reinman. She looked like she was trying to be stern but like she felt sorry for me too. "It usually means you were trying your hardest. And that's good."

I didn't say anything.

"That will be the end of the class for today, girls. We're all out of time. Let's go."

We all filed out. I wished silently that the floor would open up and swallow me whole. I could feel everybody looking at me. Even the older girls who had the next class and were watching the end of ours while they waited. As I walked by them I heard one of them say, "What, do they have affirmative action here now too?"

I spun around to say something but no words would come out. I didn't even know who had said it. They all walked in, all grace and perfection, wisps of hair tickling their necks. I could have killed them all in that second. If I'd had a gun or something, I would have. But then I looked at my hands, smooth, medium brown, mine. And I wished I could rub the color off.

I didn't say anything to Stacey as we got dressed. And I didn't say anything as we walked over to Wendy's to eat. I felt like if I opened my mouth, I'd start screaming or something. The only thing I could think of was this thing that happened when I was little. It was one of the first times my mom had sent me to the corner store to get something for her and I was walking home by myself, feeling very grown up. All of a sudden, this white kid, about the same age as me with scruffy blond hair, came up beside me and started asking me questions. What was my name? Where did I go to school? Where did I live? At first I was talking

116

to him but then I remembered I wasn't supposed to talk to strangers so I stopped and began to walk faster, finally getting past him. He didn't chase me but as I started to run away he yelled, "Is that street you live on somewhere up your ass, you nigger bitch?" My ears pounded for the rest of the day. But I never told either of my parents. Even though I knew he was wrong, not me, I felt ashamed and dirty. Just like I did now.

At lunch, Stacey looked at me gently and said, "You know, falling isn't the end of the world."

I didn't mean to—especially not in this horrible fast-food joint—but I just started crying. I could barely talk. "Oh, Stace. Somebody said something about me being there on affirmative action. I just—"

"Who said that?"

"I don't know. Somebody in the older girls' class. I can't do anything. I don't even know who said it. But now I feel like they're all thinking it. I feel like I can't dance, like I don't even belong here really. I just feel sick."

Stacey sighed and muttered, "Those evil heifers. Are you sure you don't know who said it?"

"Yeah."

"Damn. Well, look, you I can talk to. Here, look at me." I wiped my eyes and looked into her serious brown ones. "You cannot get into this school unless you can dance your ass off. Unless you're one of the best in the country, they just do *not* let you in. And it's even harder for us—not easier. So don't let those . . . I don't even know what to call them . . . those *dancers* tell you that you don't belong here. You do. We both do. Don't let them make you run. Not from what you love."

I stopped crying. I tried to take her words in, to swallow the strength in them whole. But they stuck in my throat.

I stumbled through adagio class that afternoon in a daze. I didn't fall or anything but I felt like everyone was looking at me. Josh's hands on my waist felt weird and dirty. As he supported me through a turn and I looked in his eyes I wondered, "What is he really thinking about me? Did he mean what he said about wishing I would be back next year? Does he even think I should be here now?" When I looked at the two of us in the mirror, his pale blond hair and fair skin against my dark arms and hair, I felt like a freak. I didn't even talk to him the way I usually did after class—sometimes we'd practice a tough lift or talk a little about what we'd each been working on in class, but today I just ran out as soon as it was over. I barely said good-bye to him.

Stacey cornered me in the dressing room after

class. "Are you all right, Vick? Do you want me to come home with you or anything?"

I took a deep breath. "No, I'm . . . I just need to be by myself for a little while. I'll be okay."

She looked at me suspiciously. "All right. But *call* me, would you? Call me."

I said I would. I just wanted to go home and lie on my bed and feel nothing.

*H*is apartment was amazing. It was like a big open loft. I'd never seen anything like it except in movies. What seemed like acres of warm-looking wood and small, expensive white rugs were everywhere. Photos of George Balanchine, and of Misha and other dancers in different roles were all over the walls. And a lot of books, some in Russian but most in English, like he couldn't wait to put his old life behind him once he left.

Dinner was like a dream. I saw it in parts now. The perfect food. The way he held a cigarette. His face when he was asking me a question, like he really wanted to know the answer. The way his accent softened everything he said, made it seem special and elegant and different. The way he smiled, like he was smiling at me now as we sat on the huge, soft couch.

"Two things. Would you like anything to drink? And what are you thinking about? You seem so far away."

"Me? Oh, white wine, I guess. And I'm thinking that this whole thing is kind of amazing."

"What's so amazing about it?"

"Oh, come on, Misha. You know perfectly well that every girl in the company would give up her favorite toe shoes to be sitting here. I feel like I hit the lottery or something."

Laughing, he handed me a glass of wine. "So I am a lottery prize to you girls. I don't know how I feel about this. I like to think I am just a person."

"You are a person—but you know, you must know . . ." I trailed off.

"I *am* just a person." He paused. "One who finds you very beautiful. I want you to stay here tonight. Do you want to?"

"Yes, very much," I said, afraid to look at him. It was so quiet I could hear my own breath. He looked at me intently, then took my hand.

"Come then. We have all night."

I sat on my bed, looking out at the black asphalt street and the streetlight across the way. I didn't tell Aunt Hannah what had happened at school. Just claimed a headache and hid out in my room after dinner. I think she could tell something was up but she didn't press me. So I just lay on my bed and thought about Misha for about two hours straight.

Did they really let me in only because I was black? I know in my head that they didn't. That's not how this school works; you can see it just by going through the auditions. If you can't dance, or if you're fat, or if you're sway-kneed or sway-backed or your boobs are too big or you're too short or too tall, you don't get in. You don't even make it past first cut. I know that. I know this is just the kind of thing that my mom was talking about when we drove up here, that I shouldn't let people treat me with ignorance. And that my dad would say, "Now, little girl, you know you're as good as they are. Better than some. Don't let them tell you any different." It's like what Michael was saying when he got so mad at me—they see us all the same.

So why did I still have this big lump in my stomach? It was like that girl, whoever she was, saw some secret, horrible thing about me, something in my skin, something I couldn't tell anyone. It was like the way I felt when I saw those girls on the subway. Like maybe there really was something awful about them, about us, and we were just kidding ourselves to think otherwise. My eyes burned. What would Dad say if he knew I was thinking like this? He'd be so mad. I felt mad at myself. Mad and sick and ashamed.

That's why it's safer with Misha, really. I know he'd look at me and just see me; not somebody who doesn't belong in ballet. He wouldn't think like that; he couldn't. He'd see how hard I've worked and how much I love to dance right away. And he'd appreciate it and love me for it. I wish I could find somewhere that's like that place in my head where he lives. Someplace where I'd never feel this way.

Chapter Eleven

The next morning when I woke up, my eyes were all grainy and sore. I felt like I'd been crying all night even though I really hadn't. I cried a little but mostly I just lay on my back, staring at the ceiling, feeling myself sink into the bed. Aunt Hannah was already up when I finally got up and went to the refrigerator for some juice and yogurt. I knew if I didn't eat anything, she'd get on me and I just couldn't face it. She was reading *Backstage*. I didn't say anything. The silence grew louder and louder until she finally put the paper down. "Vicki, obviously something is bothering you. I just want you to know that I'm here if you need to talk about it," she said. Her eyes were gentle and sad.

I felt the words crowd my throat but then I just couldn't. I didn't even know where to start. So I just said, "Thanks. I've got to get going. I don't want to be late." If I'd said any more, I would have started crying. So I got my dance bag, kissed her on the forehead and got out of there as fast as I could.

I could feel the heat through the soles of my shoes as I walked out the front door of the building. I watched everybody who walked by carefully. A group of white kids, maybe eleven or twelve years old, walked by me. One looked at me for a minute. My stomach tightened. Was he looking because he thought I was pretty? Or did he see me with my hair neatly caught back and my dance bag over my shoulder as some kind of accident? If I passed a bunch of other black kids would they think I was some kind of freak? I hurried to the subway station, my head down, trying not to look at people.

Class wasn't much better. Stacey and I usually tried to stand next to each other but she got there late so I didn't get to talk to her at all and I ended up being next to Debbie at the barre.

She is so good. When she's up on pointe, it's like she barely touches the ground at all, like she could take off at any minute. She looks the way I always want to feel but I only rarely do.

Taking the barre behind her was amazing. Every move was so precise. My head hurt and my

124

eyes still felt like someone had poured sand into them but I found myself holding my head a little straighter and hopping onto pointe a little more crisply just because of the way she did it.

After class, we all got to the door at the same time. Debbie spoke first: "That was some class. Miss Reinman just about worked me to death."

"That's for sure," said Stacey. "That was a tough class."

I nodded and wiped my neck with a towel. Then Debbie said, "Why don't you guys come up to my room after you get changed? We can hang out till adagio." She looked eagerly from me to Stacey. I hesitated a second and then said yes. I don't know why. I had zero desire to hang around with Debbie, but I didn't have anything else to do or the energy to come up with an excuse.

The dorms at SAB are kind of like college dorms—well, what I think college dorms would be like anyway. Except college dorms wouldn't have people sitting in splits all over the hallways. They're in a real tall building behind the school and everybody had their own room with the same brand-new furniture that looks like school furniture and scratchy, new-smelling carpet. Debbie had posters over every inch of wall space—a big picture of James Dean and pictures of Leonardo DiCaprio and Brad Pitt and old movie stills from

Rebel Without a Cause and *Splendor in the Grass*. She had one small poster from the White Oak Dance Project, Misha's modern dance company, but she didn't have any other dance stuff up. It was totally different from my room, which was covered in dance posters (mostly Misha).

Stacey and I sat on the bed and Debbie sat on the floor. In a split, of course. At first nobody knew what to say. I looked out the window and Stacey leafed through a copy of *Elle* on the bedside table. When I looked back at Debbie, she looked like she was sorry she'd thought of this whole thing.

Finally, Stacey said, "So, Deb, how are you and Henry getting along?" Henry is this guy in the boys' division. He almost always partners Debbie because they're almost the same height, but he has a lot of trouble with lifts and stuff. I'm shorter so I never get put with him, thank God. Debbie rolled her eyes. "You know how he is, Stacey. Every time he picks me up I'm just waiting to hit the floor. It's death-defying."

We all laughed. "But you know," Debbie went on, "he's not really a bad guy. I was talking to him after class the other day. He's here all the way from Oklahoma and he's never been to New York before and he's really trying. Mr. Mazo's been working with him and he's getting a little better."

"That's cool. For your sake," Stacey said.

We were all quiet for a minute. Then Debbie said, "So, who do you think is going to get asked back for the fall?"

Stacey and I just gave each other these looks. Then we turned to Debbie and said at the same time, "You!" Debbie turned bright red and shifted out of her split. "You really think so?" she said.

"Duh," said Stacey. "I *think* so. You're only the best dancer in the school. Geez, Debbie, you know that."

"Well, I don't know. My butt's too big and my turns to the left aren't all that good."

"Debbie, you're gonna get in. Don't be so dense." Stacey sounded exasperated, like they'd talked about this before. I hadn't said anything. I couldn't believe that Debbie felt this way. She was so good—and besides she looked like a dancer, all pink and white and blond. How could she not know she was going to get in? Nobody would ever make any affirmative-action crack to her. I could feel my heart beating hard under my leotard. I had to look out the window again. I couldn't look at her.

I was still looking out the window when she spoke. "So, do you guys think you're going to get in?"

My heart got louder but I couldn't open my

127

mouth. Stacey spoke first. "I don't know. I don't think my placement is solid enough."

Words left my mouth before I even knew they were coming. "That's not the only thing. It doesn't matter how much we want to do it, people are always going to think we just got in because we're black anyway!" I jumped up and ran out of the room. My mouth felt filled with salt and sorrow. I could hear both of them calling my name, Stacey chasing me down the hall but I didn't stop. I ran all the way down the stairs and didn't stop until I was standing on Lincoln Center Plaza. The breath in my ears was louder than the sounds of the street. I started walking toward Columbus, heading uptown. I didn't care where I was going. I just couldn't be still. And I couldn't stay there.

I just walked and walked. I don't even know how long it was. Car horns were honking and the pavement shimmered with heat but I just kept walking, all the way up to Central Park and into it. Finally, I flopped under a tree. I could feel the sweat running down my back. A pebble dug into my thigh but I didn't move. I knew I was missing adagio class but I didn't move. I just lay there, looking up through the branches, watching the light change and shift over me. I kept imagining Misha's hair under my hands, the things he would say to me. "Don't worry about those girls," he'd say. "They know nothing. I know. I can see that you belong here. You are a wonderful dancer." He took me in his arms gently. "You're a wonderful dancer. Your skin, it's nothing, it doesn't matter. It only matters that you love dancing and you do it well. That's what matters."

I finally sat up as the sounds of the park began to fade and the sunlight above me changed to cool amber. I looked at my watch and jumped up. It was nearly five-thirty. If I didn't get home soon, Aunt Hannah would think I'd been mugged or something. I practically ran to the subway.

When I got back to the building, I stopped outside to run my hands over my face and check my hair. I didn't want to have to explain things to Aunt Hannah. I just felt like it would be easier to say I'd been at class. As soon as I walked in, she kissed me quickly on the forehead and said, "Stacey called. She said you should call her back as soon as you can."

"Okay. Can I use the phone in your room?"

"Sure."

I knew Stacey wouldn't leave me alone so I figured I might as well call her back and get it over with. She picked up right away. "Vick, are you okay? I couldn't even think in class I was so worried. Are you all right?"

"I'm fine. I'm fine."

"Uh, yeah. Screaming at Debbie and running out like that is just fine. Vick, you've gotta talk to me. What can I do?"

"Nothing. What can you do? I feel like garbage. What can you do?" I paused. "Debbie probably thinks the same thing."

Stacey pulled in her breath sharply. "Thanks. Thanks a lot. You think I'd hang around with someone who'd think something like that?"

"I don't know. I don't know what she thinks."

"Yeah, well, I do. We talked for a long time after you went tearing out. She was just as mad as I am. Just as mad as you should be. Vicki, whoever said that was just mean and full of nastiness. She doesn't see who you really are. You can't let her tell you who you are. Don't you see that?"

I was quiet for a long time. "I guess I don't," I finally said.

"Well, you better," said Stacey. I didn't know what to say after that. The words didn't exist.

Chapter Twelve

Aunt Hannah always gets *The New York Times* and the *Daily News*. She says that way she gets the trash and the class all at once. The *News* is one of those tabloid papers with big, blocky headlines. If you read it enough, you think the whole city is going to blow up at any second. I like to look at it for the comics and Ann Landers but I always flip through the *Times*. It's a big paper and it seems very full of itself—but they have much more stuff about ballet.

I had managed to pull myself together enough that Aunt Hannah wasn't asking any questions. Which was fine with me. We were sitting at the breakfast table, not talking, pushing the papers back and forth, when I saw it. A giant picture of Misha. Big as life. He was going to be at Macy's. He has this line of dancewear, leotards and stuff

131

that have his name on them. I have some of the tights. He was going to be there to promote it. Today. I couldn't even breathe. I could go there, see him, maybe even touch him or talk to him. My head started to buzz as I stared at the picture. "Vicki." Aunt Hannah's voice made me look up. "Do you want some more orange juice?"

"Huh? Oh, no thanks, Aunt Hannah. Listen, I've gotta get going, I'm going to be late for class."

"But you haven't even finished eating."

"I know, I'm sorry. I forgot I needed to be early today. I'll have an extra-big lunch, okay?"

Aunt Hannah looked skeptical. "You'd better. All right, I guess you should go if you've got to go."

I ran back into the bedroom, grabbed the earrings I'd bought in SoHo and the lipstick that Stacey and I had bought one day after class and ran out, kissing Aunt Hannah quickly. She had that "what's going on" look that grown-ups get when they want to ask you something but aren't sure they should. I just looked right back in her eyes and said, "I'll be home at the usual time. Everything's fine."

I walked to the subway in a daze. He was going to be at Macy's at eleven-thirty. It was a brilliant, sunny day and everything seemed to shimmer even more than usual. I walked past the guy who's always asking for money on the corner and gave him fifty cents without hesitating. I wanted everyone to be as excited as I was. The last two days seemed like some kind of distant nightmare; everything was different now. I was going to have to skip class that morning but it would be worth it. To meet Misha; to have him finally see me—it was worth anything. I took the train straight to Macy's. I didn't want to have to answer a lot of questions at school and I didn't have much time. It was already ten-forty-five.

The store was mobbed. There were about a million sales going on and people wearing shorts, clutching bathing suits and maroon Macy's bags raced everywhere. But they had a sign right as you came in that said COME MEET MIKHAIL BARYSH-NIKOV IN INTIMATES ON 6 *TODAY* AT 11:30. So I hadn't misread the ad. He was probably upstairs now, waiting. My knees started shaking. I needed to find the bathroom and put some lipstick on.

I fought my way past the counters full of glossy stockings and leather wallets and smooth silky scarves to the bathroom on the sixth floor. There was a line out the door and the women in it gave me dirty looks as I walked in. "I'm just using the mirror," I called, and people immediately looked less angry. Once I got in front of the mirror, I looked at myself for a long minute. People always called me cute but I didn't want to be cute. I wanted to be devastating, sophisticated, stunning. I leaned forward to put on the lipstick. When I finished, I looked older, but still like me. Short of some speedy plastic surgery, there was nothing else I could do. I checked the sides of my hair and added a little more gel. Then, with a deep breath, I went out to get on line.

It was unbelievably crowded. Old guys with feathery white hair and delicately wrinkled skin clutched copies of the big photo books *Baryshnikov at Work* and *Private View;* brittle mothers and daughters from Queens with Noo Yawk accents and stiff, tall hair stood chatting to each other, clutching old American Ballet Theatre programs and looking around wildly every time there was the slightest movement in the crowd. And lots of other dancers like me, only none of them were black. But we were like a tribe, with our smoothed flat hair and our turned-out feet. How would he know me, know that I was special among all these people? I imagined how he'd look, signing things quickly with a nod here, an obliging smile there. Polite and professional, but just as perfect and beautiful as I always knew he would be. As I move toward the front of the line, I can hear my heart in my ears, hammering away. Then he looks up at me, those blue eyes friendly, but not really there, thinking about who's next in line, how many more to go, until he really sees me. Then he's genuinely interested.

I touch my earrings and say, "My name's Vicki Harris. I really love your work. I'm studying dance at SAB."

"That's good. When I saw you, I said to myself. 'Ah, now here is a dancer'." He looks quickly down the line. "Look, there are so many people here. Why don't I sign this for you, but here, give me your phone number. I will call you. You look like a remarkable dancer." He smiles. "And an interesting person." All I can see is the blue of his eyes.

I was so lost in imagining what it would be like that I jumped when music started booming out of the speakers. Everybody started shoving forward but I got into a position where I could just barely see what was happening. I could see slinky models prancing down the runway, bright, fake smiles on their faces. The clothes were okay—a lot of flared-leg catsuits and leotards and jogbras. I couldn't believe he really had anything to do with designing

135

them. It seemed a little cheesy—and he couldn't possibly need the money. It bothered me a little.

The music seemed to last for hours, although I guess it was really only about twenty minutes. Finally the last note died out and a harsh metallic voice boomed out. "Ladies and gentlemen, Mr. Mikhail Baryshnikov!"

I shoved my way to the front of the clot of people I was in, my tongue pushed hard against my teeth. There he was, walking coolly down the aisle between two models. They were both taller than he was. He was wearing a perfectly cut, rust-colored suit and his hair was cut short and sticking up a little bit, stylishly. Each movement he made was perfect, smooth, economical, like everything was run by a small, well-oiled machine inside him. He made the models look clunky and ungraceful. He was smiling a little bit, the way he had in so many of my dreams.

The models led him to a small table and he sat behind it, grinning and never once blinking as thousands of camera flashes went off in his face, each one a tiny star of light. The models shifted and posed behind him, throwing their hair around, but he kept smiling and he never moved. I was transfixed. I honestly thought that I could die, right there and be happy. Just to have seen him. To know that I would move even closer to him was some kind of dream. A woman with efficient steel-gray hair and a gold Macy's pin handed him a pen and the line began to move forward. The store was handing out posters with his picture on them but people gave him different things to sign—books, old dance programs, posters of their own. Some people took pictures of him with their own small cameras. He smiled obligingly at everyone, but not like he meant it. He turned to the next person almost before the one in front of him was gone.

My mouth got drier and drier as I moved forward on the line. I never looked away from him. Now there were three people in front of me, now two, now one. Now I was standing in front of him.

In books, blue eyes are always described as the color of sky, the color of cornflowers, but I never thought I'd see any like that. Until this. They were lit from within. His face was lined, not young, not boyish. And those dark circles under his eyes were still there. His hands on the pen were muscular, used to working, to holding on to a barre, but the nails were neat and buffed-looking. He looked a little tired. I stood there for a second. I couldn't talk. "What's your name?" he finally asked, in that accented voice I knew so well.

"Vicki, I . . ."

He pulled a poster over with a quick, elegant flourish and signed it "To Vickie. Best, Mikhail Baryshnikov" without ever looking at me. He shoved it toward me, those blue, blue eyes, polite, walled-off, distant, looking toward the next person on line and the next and the next after that. I still didn't move. The gray-haired woman shoved the poster at me again and out of the corner of my eye, I saw a security guard step toward me. My feet unstuck and I stepped away, my eyes hot, my throat closed. He didn't even see me. He didn't even want to talk to me. There was nothing between us at all. I looked at the poster. He'd spelled my name wrong.

My eyes filled with tears, right there in the middle of Intimates. The ground beneath my feet seemed to shift, no longer something I could trust. I walked through the store not seeing anything. The weird thing was, I was thinking about my dad. One time, not long before he left, we were all at dinner. I could tell that Ma and Dad had been arguing but they weren't talking about it in front of us. He looked at me—at all of us really—with that same polite, walled-off look in his eyes. Like he had to be nice to us, but we were really a roomful of strangers. It wasn't always like that. When I was really little, just four or five, we used to go on long walks, just him and me. I'd tell him about school; how Mrs. Lapsley had given me a gold star and said I was the best reader, or how me and my friend Sheila were going to live on the moon someday. He listened to all of it like I was the smartest, funniest person in the world.

He liked to take me over to Rutgers, where he taught, and show me around the library. "See," he'd say, "those numbers tell you how to find whatever book you want." He'd pull down a book—one I remember is *Not Without Laughter* by Langston Hughes—and show it to me. He loved being around books; his face almost glowed in their presence. And he loved sharing them with me, helping me see what it was he loved. When I started taking ballet, there wasn't time for all that anymore. And then he started fighting with Ma, and then we just couldn't talk at all.

Somehow, I managed to find the escalator and get to the first floor, clutching the poster. I pushed past all the people—they looked ugly to me now. I wanted to cry again when I thought about how happy I had been when I first came in.

I went home. I didn't know what else to do. I cried all the way on the subway. Not bawling my head off or anything, but I couldn't stop the tears from running down my face. I wiped them with the back of my hand. People looked at me funny but no one said anything. I kept staring at a

Planned Parenthood ad on the subway wall opposite me. I finally dug around in my dance bag until I found an old napkin from Wendy's to wipe my eyes with.

I let myself in with the key Aunt Hannah had given me for emergencies. The apartment was cool and quiet, empty. I stood by the door for a minute. Then it was like I was hit by a truck. I barely walked into the room. I didn't even put down my dance bag or the poster. All of a sudden, I was crumpled on the floor sobbing. I could hear my voice from far away saying "Why is this happening?" over and over. Then no words, just moans. I don't know how long I sat there bawling, almost shrieking sometimes. Until I couldn't cry anymore. I felt like the only person left on the planet. I had just dragged myself into the living room and was sitting on the sofa, snuffling, my mind blank, when Aunt Hannah came into the living room. I hadn't even heard her come in.

She looked scared when she saw me. "Vicki? What on earth? What happened, hon? Did somebody try to hurt you?"

"I . . . no, nothing like that. I just . . ."

She put her stuff down and sat next to me. "Take a deep breath and tell me what happened."

Her eyes were fixed on mine. It was all I could do just to answer her. "Okay. I . . . I didn't go to class this morning. You know I really like Baryshnikov, right?"

"Sure. He's a wonderful dancer."

"I went to Macy's today. He was there, like promoting some stupid clothes that have his name on them. I wanted, I just wanted to meet him, to get a chance to talk to him. I waited and waited on line but then when I got up there . . . I was standing right in front of him and I couldn't even talk. He didn't even look at me. I don't know. I know it's stupid but I thought . . . I thought he'd see me. That he'd want to talk to me."

Aunt Hannah looked at me quietly for a long time after I finished. I was waiting for her to tell me how stupid I was, how he was old enough to be my father and how nobody like him would be interested in me. But she didn't. "This meant a lot to you, huh?"

"It meant everything."

She looked away from me for a minute, like she might cry herself. "Did I ever tell you how I decided to become an actress? God, I remember it like it was yesterday. I went to the movies—with your mother, actually. We used to go to the movies all the time. It was snowing really hard out and we went to see *The Godfather*. Al Pacino. It was the first time I'd ever seen him in anything. My God. At the end of it, I couldn't even move. I'd never seen a performance like that in my life. It was everything acting was about. Your mom didn't feel the same way I did, but I knew when I left the theater that day that I would do anything to be a part of that. If I could be half as good, I'd die happy. Later, after I'd started acting myself, I ended up at this party he was at." She laughed and threw her head back suddenly, remembering. "It took me *three* days to decide what to wear. I paid my rent late so I could get a new dress. So finally, here I am at this party, my hair done up, my makeup perfect, and he comes in with this gorgeous woman on his arm. Everybody's hovering around him. He's the most famous person there. But I managed to shove my way to the front and stammer out something. I think I said that I really loved *The Godfather*."

"And then what happened? Did he talk to you?"

Aunt Hannah looked at me and smiled sadly. "Not at all. He said thank you with his eyes looking straight over my head. Then he went to get a drink. I never saw him again." She paused and when she spoke again, her voice was still gentle but harder somehow. "But I'm still here."

I started crying again. "I feel like I'm going to die, Aunt Hannah."

"I know, I know," she said softly. "And I know

you don't believe me but you're not going to die. You can't. I'd miss you too much."

She pulled me close to her on the sofa and stroked my hair while I cried, like I was just a little kid. We sat there like that for a while. Finally, I spoke. "There's something else I wanted to tell you. About this girl in my school."

"Yeah? What is it, punkin?"

"This girl, a couple of days ago, I don't know who it was, she said"—I started crying harder—"she said I was just there because of affirmative action. Like I didn't belong at the school at all."

Aunt Hannah's hand stopped stroking my hair for a minute. I could feel her body stiffen. Then she sighed. "Oh, Vicki, hon, I'm so sorry. And I'm so sorry that you felt like you couldn't tell me. I know Alicia and Jason have tried to raise you so you'd know how full of crap a girl like that is. But I can see, I've been seeing all summer how you've been struggling with it. I know it must seem like they have to be right. Everybody's white—you're the only one who's not. Why shouldn't you believe them? Maybe you don't belong. Is that what you've been thinking?"

My breath caught in my throat. "Yes," I said. My voice was very small.

"You know, you and I are a lot alike, punkin. We both love professions that don't make much room for people like us. And we talk a good game, we say we know we belong because that's what we're supposed to say, but sometimes late at night, when it's quiet, we both start wondering if that's true. I wish there was an easy solution. I wish people weren't so damn narrow-minded. I wish you didn't have to go through this. But the only way through it is through it. One day, you'll wake up and Baryshnikov will seem like a dream you had, just like Al is for me. I'll always have a soft spot for him but now, my acting is about me, not about him, not about impressing a lot of white people or convincing them I have a right to do this. It's for me. That's going to happen for you too. I know it. But I know it's hard now, punkin. Please believe that I know how hard it is. And remember you've always got somebody you can count on right here." She paused and laughed a little. "There's a reason we're both so crazy about these white boys we'll never know. It's when we stop being so crazy that we can do our best work, though." She stopped talking, but her hand started moving over my hair again, soft and gentle. After a little while she said, "That was a lot, I know. And it was probably hard to hear. Are you okay?"

"Okay. Not great, but okay." I sniffled.

"Well, that's what counts. I love you, Vicki."

"I love you too, Aunt Hannah."

She pulled me to her a little tighter. We sat like that for a long time. There didn't seem to be anything else to say.

Chapter Thirteen

You know how it feels when you're swimming and you decide to see how long you can stay under? You fill your cheeks with air and float in the aimless, humming blue until your cheeks start to swell and your lungs hurt and you start pushing your arms to get to the top and when you finally make it and the surface of the water breaks away all around you and you draw that first sweet breath and your mind is washed clear. That's what it was like when I told Aunt Hannah about Misha and about that girl's remark. But telling her and having her not make fun of me or tell me I was being crazy made me feel, I don't know, more grown-up, more like a real person I guess. I had been so afraid to tell anybody; I was so ashamed and felt so stupid. But Aunt Hannah had treated me kindly and now I felt safer.

It was weird, though. My head felt empty for those first few days after I saw Misha at the store. At home after class I would lie on my bed and try to think about him the way I had just a week before but I couldn't. It felt fake, on some kind of dead frequency. Whenever I'd try to call his face up in my mind, to think about how I thought we'd dance together, I'd only get the cold blue way that he looked past me to everyone else in the line. Then I'd get a vision of my eyes filling with tears, me running out of the store. I couldn't think after that. I'd just roll onto my stomach and cry into my pillow.

I was so busy being sad that I even managed to forget that I had asked Michael to go to the ballet with me until he called me a couple of days before. I was just lying on my bed, feeling my feet throb and looking at the ceiling when the phone rang. It was him. "Yo, Vick. What's up? What time we gotta get together on Sunday?"

"Oh my God, that's right. We're supposed to go to the ballet on Sunday."

"You forgot?" he said. His voice went up a little, disappointed.

My voice came out rushed and apologetic. "I'm sorry, Michael. I still really want to go but I did forget. I . . . I've been extra busy this week." Busy having my heart broken, I thought.

"Dag. How busy could you be? What have you been doing?" he said.

"Well, we were learning a new variation in class and my aunt had me doing all this stuff and . . . I still want to go. I didn't forget because I didn't want to go." That last part was true. It felt weird to have such a big thing going on in my head that I didn't want to talk to him about but I don't think he would get it about Misha. I can't really see any boy understanding it. So I didn't say anything about that.

He was quiet a moment. "You're sure you still want to go?" he finally said. His voice sounded small, like he was afraid I'd start yelling at him or something. Like he was afraid I'd been thinking about it and decided I didn't like him so much after all.

"Yes. I really still want to go." I was holding the phone so tight that my hand hurt. I could feel it in my knuckles.

When he spoke this time, it was as if he'd made up his mind about something. "All right then. What time should I come by?"

"Around quarter to one, I guess. The performance is at two. We could do something after if you want."

"Cool. I'll come get you. You sure everything's all right?"

"Yeah, yeah, I'm fine. It'll be fun to see you. I'll see you Sunday, okay?"

I slid down the wall to sit on the floor after I hung up. My head felt very clear, and full of light. I did want to see Michael. I didn't feel the same floating, dizzy feeling that I had about Misha, though. It seemed more real, like the way I feel after landing a jump well. Like this is something I can really do. It's something I really love. The wall felt very solid behind my back.

On Sunday, Michael showed up right on time. He was wearing a gray suit with a yellow striped tie and clutching a bunch of daisies. Nobody had ever given me flowers before. I took them, but I couldn't look at him. Instead I looked back at Aunt Hannah, who stood in the hall doorway watching us. "God. Thanks, Michael. Thanks a lot," I said. If I'd been white, my face would have been totally red, I was blushing so hard. "Why don't I take those and put them in water so they'll be fresh when you get home," said Aunt Hannah. Her lips were pressed together like she was trying not to smile. "All right. You guys have a good time and I'll see you in a few hours. Okay?"

We both said goodbye and left. When we got to the street I said, "The flowers were beautiful, Michael. Really. Nobody ever gave me flowers before."

"You deserved them." He paused. "You look real nice."

My face got hot again and I looked away from him. "Thanks. Thanks a lot."

We were down in the subway now, and the train came right away. "This must be my lucky day," Michael said as we ran across the platform to get on. Once we got seats, neither of us seemed to know what to say. We both stared at the ads above us. At Ninety-sixth Street, a dark-skinned guy got on wearing baggy jeans and a Notre Dame hat. He smiled when he saw us and came over, grinning. "Hey, Mike. What up, G.?"

"Yo, what's up, man? Where you going?"

"I'm going down to Seventy-second to get some stuff for school. Where are you going? And aren't you going to introduce me?"

Michael looked mortified. "Oh man, I'm sorry. Jamal, this is Vicki. Vicki, Jamal. We're going to the ballet." He lifted his chin a little as he said this, like he was daring Jamal to say anything about it.

"You're Vicki? Oh man, I've heard a lot about you," Jamal said, a big smile on his face. Then he looked back at Michael for a minute. "The ballet, huh? Well, I guess love makes you do foolish things." He looked up. "This is my stop. Have a good time, y'all." He jumped off the train.

Michael was looking steadily at his shoes when I asked him, "You've been talking about me?"

"Yeah. Yeah, I have."

"God. Well, that's nice."

Michael didn't say anything. I scowled a little, suddenly. "Do you think going to the ballet's a foolish thing?"

He looked up, and straight at me. "You love it, so I'm willing to check it out." We were at our stop. He touched my back lightly as we got up to get off the train.

$\mathcal{L}$incoln Center was swirling with colors. It was a perfect summer day for once, not too hot or humid. Everybody was hanging out on the plaza eating ice cream bars and leaning on the edge of the fountain. Little kids chased each other, wearing their ruffly, dressed-up best clothes. Michael's eyes widened as we walked across the plaza. "Man, this is really something. You come here every day?"

"Well, not here. But I take ballet class right over there." I pointed to the school, back behind the plaza. "It doesn't look like this every day. Usually there aren't people all over the place."

"Still. This is something." He looked at me for a minute, like he was a little scared of me or something. "Every day, huh? That's really cool."

I could feel myself blushing as I said, "Come on, let's go in."

The student seats were way up in the fourth ring so they weren't great but they weren't the worst we could get either. The program was good, though. *Apollo, Glass Pieces* and *The Four Temperaments*—I'd seen *The Four Temperaments* before and Debbie and some of the other girls at the school said that the other ones were great too. Michael flipped through his program with a doubtful look on his face until the lights went down.

Every time I go to the ballet, it hits me again. Even if it isn't Misha dancing I can barely breathe during the performance. It's just so beautiful, watching them float through space, imagining these perfect dancers counting to themselves in their heads, feeling each move as they go along. The music, the dancing, the lights—it's all so perfect. In a weird way, it's always like that time I saw *The Nutcracker*. Moving like that, being a part of it, seems to me the only thing a person could really want to do with their life. I don't know. That sounds silly but it's really how I feel when I'm watching them.

Halfway through *Glass Pieces*, that one where there are so many dancers crisscrossing each other toward the end, I found myself watching the only girl in the corps who was black. I'd known she was there, but we didn't really see company members all that much so I'd never seen her before. Her hair was neat and smooth just like everyone else's. Even though I could see her and realized that she looked a little different from the other girls, it wasn't bad. She stuck out—but not in a bad way. I thought of what the minister had said at Michael's church about not being ashamed. And all that stuff Aunt Hannah had said about not trying to prove it all the time. Just being the best I could be and not letting them tell me who I was. That must be what this girl had to do. And there she was. Onstage with NYCB. There might be a place for me after all. I applauded my head off at the end. So did Michael.

"I really liked it," he said as we went down the stairs crowded with people. "I wouldn't have come to something like this on my own but it was all right. I love the way they look all up on their toes. Can you do all that stuff?"

"Me? I wish. I mean, it's ballet, the same thing I'm studying, but no, I don't dance like that. Not even close."

"I bet you're better than you think."

"Some people say that to me—but I never believe it."

He looked at me seriously. "You should." I didn't know what to say to that so I didn't say anything. We had walked over to the fountain and were leaning against it. He looked over at the people still pouring out the doors of the theater. "I can't believe you just come up here all the time like it's no big deal," he said softly. Then abruptly, his tone changed, became louder, less like he was scared. "Listen, you wanna walk over to Columbus for a little while? Walk around, look in stores and stuff?"

"Yeah, that would be fun."

We started walking over. We didn't talk much—Michael's words about me being better than I thought reverberated in my head. He seemed so serious. It was like he wasn't talking only about dancing. It was weird to feel how different we were, the different worlds we moved in—I didn't know anybody like his friend Jamal. And he seemed so impressed, intimidated even, by me hanging around Lincoln Center all the time. It *was* still a big deal to me but not in the way it was to him. Even the way we spoke was so different. But I liked him anyway. Lately nothing was what I hoped it would be. Misha didn't think I was special; Michael did. And it felt okay.

Columbus Avenue is where a lot of the coolest stores are. You can spend a whole day walking up and down, wandering in and out, trying stuff on. I'd been there with Stacey but never with a guy before. The first place we went to was the Gap, of course. He held up a sleeveless cotton sundress, grinning. "This would look good on you."

"Yeah? You wanna buy it for me?"

"Oh sure. Didn't I tell you Wendy's pays me a hundred and fifty dollars an hour? I'm a rich man. Anything you want in here, baby, it's yours," he said, sweeping his arm around to take in the whole store.

I cracked up. "You're crazy," I finally sputtered.

"Yeah, that's what they tell me. Let's get out of here."

We walked along a little farther and came to a men's clothing store. The window display was just a pair of buttery-looking loafers, soft hazel-colored pants and a silk shirt that made you think of the word *perfect*. "Now this is the stuff I like. That designer stuff," said Michael.

"You can pay for it with that big money from Wendy's."

He looked at me, his eyes bright. "Wanna go in?"

"They'll know we can't buy anything."

"So? We're allowed to look, aren't we?" We looked at each other for a minute, then headed for the door. Michael pulled on it but it didn't open. Then I tried. "Hey, wait, there's a doorbell here.

155

Let me buzz it," I said, leaning on it. The clerks inside were all women so blond their hair was almost white. Their clothes were all black and they looked at Michael and me with big frightened eyes for just a second before turning defiantly back to filling out order slips and helping other customers. I turned to Michael, confused. "What's going on? I don't . . ." I trailed off when I saw his face, knotted and angry. I had a terrible feeling in my stomach, just like when that girl said that thing about affirmative action.

"Come on. Let's get the hell out of here," he said, his voice low and furious.

He walked off, a little ahead of me, not paying attention to whether I was on the outside or the inside of the curb. "Michael, I don't . . . What happened?"

He stopped and wheeled around in the middle of the sidewalk. People veered away from us on both sides. "Dag, girl. Were you born yesterday? You know why they wouldn't let us in. You just don't want to believe it. You just want to believe you can do that ballet mess and hang around those people and everything is okey-doke. It's not. They wouldn't let us in there because we're black, okay? They were afraid I'd trash their precious store or steal something or some bullshit like that. Damnit. Damnit. I hate that." He looked like he was going to cry. He was right, I did know why they hadn't let us in—I just didn't want to believe it. Not again. We just stood there. For a long minute. I didn't know what to say. Finally, I said, "Come on. Come with me to the park for a minute." He just looked at me, but then he turned and followed.

We didn't say a word all the way over there. Michael's face was knotted like a fist. My throat felt closed off. I knew what I wanted to say but I wasn't ready to talk yet. Finally, we found a patch of grass off away from other people and sat down. I took a deep breath. "Michael?"

"What?"

"I know how you feel." I told him about that girl and her stupid mean affirmative-action remark. "I wanted to kill her. I wanted to kill all of them. I hated her—and I didn't even know which one she was," I said finally. My eyes stung again just talking about it.

Michael looked at me, his eyes dark and serious. "Don't you get sick of this mess? I mean, every damn time I get on the subway, people look at me funny, like I'm gonna rob 'em or mug 'em or some shit. I'm sorry. I shouldn't swear in front of you."

"That's okay. I've heard it before."

"Anyway. I just get sick of it. They act like I

ain't even got a right to be walking around with them. I can't even come into their stupid stores. Damn. They make me sick."

We fell silent. I moved a little closer and took his hand, for once not thinking should I or shouldn't I? It just seemed like the right thing to do. I looked at our hands together for a minute—his dark, even brown, mine a little lighter, like coffee with cream. They looked good together. Better, I thought a little sadly, than Misha and I would have looked together. And he probably wouldn't understand what Michael and I were feeling now either. I can't hate—I don't hate anybody. But I do get sick of it, just like Michael. He sighed suddenly and smiled at me a little bit, but he still looked sad and angry. "I'm sorry you had to see this," he said softly. "But I'm glad you were here."

"Yeah. Me too."

Chapter Fourteen

A couple of days after that I was walking toward
the subway behind this group of girls and two
little babies. They were a lot like girls you see all
over the city, like the ones I saw on the train when
I first moved here. Their hair was up in elaborate
waxed shapes and they were wearing baggy jeans
and big earrings. I used to walk around girls like
that, feeling embarrassed. But this time was different. I didn't talk to them or anything but I smiled
at one girl's baby and he gurgled back at me. Then
he dropped his pacifier—he'd been clutching it—
and I bent quickly to pick it up. "Here you go," I
said, more to his mother than to him. She
smiled—she didn't look much older than me.
"Thanks. I swear, this boy would drop his own
head if it wasn't attached to his shoulders," she
said with a laugh. I smiled back and they all

walked off. She jammed the dirty pacifier into her jeans pocket and carefully adjusted the baby's hat as she walked. I stood for a second, watching them. That thing about your head being attached to your shoulders is something my mom always says. I remembered the scared face of the clerk in the store and thought how me and these girls would all get treated badly by some people, just because of our skin. They didn't deserve it any more than I did. I think that's what my parents have always wanted me to understand.

The summer was almost over. The days were a little shorter and the light had the golden, sleepy quality that means school is starting again soon. I was dancing a lot better. Still not what I saw in my head but I could feel that I was better—surer on pointe and moving more easily. There were a lot of girls better than me, though. We'd be finding out soon who would be invited back for the fall. I was not sure if I was going to be one of them.

My birthday is August fifteenth, just a week before I had to go back home. At the end of July Aunt Hannah had said to me, "What would you like for your birthday? You're going to be fifteen after all. We should celebrate in style."

I thought about it. "You know, Aunt Hannah, I'd really love to just have a party here. Mom and Beth could come up for it and Stacey and Debbie could come." I paused. "And Michael. I'd like him to come."

Aunt Hannah was quiet for a minute. "Do you want to ask your father?"

My throat closed up. "Yeah. Yeah, I do. But will him and my mom be able to sit in the same room without fighting? That's why I left him off the list. I don't want them ruining my whole birthday."

Aunt Hannah looked serious when she said, "You know, Vicki, I can't control what they do. But I do know that they wouldn't want to ruin your birthday for anything. Do you want to take a chance? See what happens?"

I decided to.

The next day Aunt Hannah said, "Vicki, I've talked to both of them. They're both going to come and they will behave. They've both promised me—and they know what I do when somebody breaks a promise to me. So you're in the clear." She hugged me briefly. "You're going to have a good birthday, okay?"

"Okay."

On the morning of my birthday, I woke up to the sun in my eyes. I wasn't thinking about Misha at all when I woke up. My fifteenth year was starting without Misha. I never thought I'd be without him. I felt a little sad. But then Aunt Hannah burst into the room with a small wrapped box, singing "Happy Birthday." She has a really amazing voice; she understudied in *Dreamgirls* for a while on Broadway. She belted out the finish like Aretha Franklin and handed me the box, smiling. I opened it. Lying on blue velvet was a gold necklace with two little gold toe shoes dangling from the ends. "Oh Aunt Hannah, it's beautiful!" I said. "Help me put it on." We put it on right over the T-shirt I sleep in. "I'll wear it forever. Thanks so much." I gave her a big hug.

"You better get up, Miss Prima Ballerina," she said, laughing. Your guests will be here in a few hours and we've got some cleaning up to do."

I was vacuuming right by the phone when it rang. I picked it up. An off-key voice, my mom's, sang "Happy Birthday" all the way through. I was laughing by the time she finished. "Happy Birthday, baby," she said. "Listen, we're just about to take off but I wanted you to hear that special solo version you always get before the party."

"Thanks, Ma."

"And listen. This is your day. Don't worry about your father and me. We talked and it's going to be okay."

"Okay?" My voice jumped up to a squeak.

My mother's voice was soft when she answered.

"It's going to be okay for today, I mean. We can be together for you without fighting. And we both love you very much. I'm sorry. I didn't want you to think . . . anything else."

"Oh." I was quiet a minute. "Well, I'm really glad you're both coming. It's going to be really fun."

"I know it will be, baby. Listen, Beth and I better get in the car or we'll never make it. See you in a little while, lovebug."

I hung up and turned the vacuum back on. She always called me lovebug when I was little but I hadn't heard it in a long time. It made me feel like she really did still love me, even when things got messed up. I started singing to myself as I pushed the vacuum around the corners of the room.

That afternoon, my dad was the first to arrive. I got the door. It felt weird to hear his voice through the buzzer. I hadn't seen him since the beginning of the summer. When he got up the stairs and I opened the door to let him in, I felt almost surprised that he looked the same. His glasses rested near the end of his nose just like they always did and he smelled of pipe smoke and chalk. "Happy Birthday, hon," he said, jamming a small wrapped package into my hand. Then he gave me a big hug and said, "How are you? I'm glad to see you." I couldn't mumble back—I could barely breathe.

By this time Aunt Hannah had come out of the kitchen where she was madly cooking up her special jerk chicken. The whole house smelled of sharp spices and heat. "Jason. It's good to see you," she said, wiping her hands on a dishtowel. He hugged her too. "Yeah, I know, Hannah. It's been too long."

"Well, sit down. You want something to drink?"

"Just a cranberry juice would be fine."

She got us both big glasses of cranberry juice and we talked for a few minutes—I told them how my classes had been going, stuff like that. My dad interrupted after a while and said, "Vicki, I can't believe how you've grown up this summer. You just seem like a whole different person."

A whole different person. I was kind of happy to hear that the way I was feeling showed. I felt different, like I'd lost something. But it didn't feel all bad. Anyway, I didn't think it showed. I smiled and said, "Thanks," to my dad. Just then the buzzer went off again. When I opened the door, Stacey and Debbie were there. "Happy Birthday," they both said at once. I laughed. "Come in, you guys." I introduced them to my father, who shook their hands like they were grown women. Debbie and Stacey looked impressed. My father's always very polite and a little formal, even with my friends. I'm used to it but I guess it would seem cool to somebody else. Debbie came up to my elbow and said, "So you wanna give me the tour? I've never been here before."

I took her back to my room, pointing out other rooms and Aunt Hannah's pictures of herself in different parts as we went. I felt like a game-show hostess as I opened the door to my room with a flourish. Debbie stepped in ahead of me.

"Wow. This is really nice. You're lucky you've got your aunt here and you didn't have to stay in the dorms."

"Yeah, I guess."

She looked quickly at my millions of Baryshnikov posters. I hadn't wanted to take them down, even though everything had changed. "You're a Baryshnikov fan, huh?"

"Yeah, I am."

"Me too. I saw him dance once a few years ago. He was *amazing*."

"You're lucky."

"Yeah." She looked at me for a minute like she wanted to say something else, then took a deep breath. "You know, the other day."

"Forget it. I was upset," I said quickly.

"I know you were, but you should have been. That girl was just an idiot. I was so mad when Stacey told me. I don't know how you felt but I just want you to know that I don't feel that way. I hope you get asked back for the fall but even if you don't . . . well, that girl was just stupid. You're a good dancer."

"God. Thanks. Thanks a lot." So Stacey was right—Debbie didn't think the same thing the rest of them did. It didn't make it hurt less but it helped. And she thought I was a good dancer too. I was pleased but I didn't know what else to say. I just stood there grinning. "Want to go back out?" I asked. She smiled and nodded.

When we got back to the living room, Michael was standing there talking to my dad. I hadn't really thought about it but he wasn't that much shorter than my dad. They didn't look much alike—they were both dark-skinned but that was all. Still they seemed alike for the few minutes I stood there before Michael came over to me and said, "Happy Birthday," and gave me a quick, embarrassed peck on the cheek. "Hi. You met everybody already, huh?" I said.

"Yep. Your pops is cool."

"That's what they tell me." I grinned. "He's all right."

"Your moms and your sister aren't here yet, huh?"

"Nope. They'll be here soon, though."

On cue, the doorbell rang and Aunt Hannah let Beth and my mom in, with a lot of fussing and kissing and stuff. My mom seemed to stand in the doorway for a minute, checking out the scene. Then she came in.

I could see her looking at my dad like a stranger. They hadn't seen each other in what?—at least five months. They both stood there for a minute. I thought of cats about to pounce, their tails flicking back and forth. Then my dad took a step toward her and my mom didn't back away. Instead she moved a little toward him and they kissed, stiffly, on the cheek. "How are you, Jason?"

"Good, Alicia. And you?"

"Keeping well, keeping well."

The air was crackling. I felt like I couldn't breathe until they both turned and my dad started talking to Aunt Hannah. My mom and Beth came over to me. "Happy birthday, baby. It's sure nice to see you," my mom said.

"Yeah, happy birthday," said Beth. Her eyes were large and she looked as nervous as I felt knowing my parents were in the same room together.

"It's nice to see you guys too." My ears were still humming and I could feel my shoulders all hunched up. "Do you want some juice or anything?"

"No, I'm fine. This must be Michael." She smiled broadly, that I-can't-wait-to-meet-you smile. Out of the corner of my eye I saw him quickly wipe his hand down his pant leg before he shook my mother's hand. "It's very nice to meet you, Mrs. Harris." I could tell she was impressed by his good manners; her smile got even bigger and her voice dropped a little, the way it does when she's pleased.

He shook Beth's hand too. She giggled and shuffled her feet as he introduced himself, then said, "Vick, come show me where to put this stuff," pointing at the two presents at her feet by the sofa. "Do you think Mom and Dad are gonna get back together?" she asked in a stage whisper as we put the gifts on the table.

"No, goofball, no way."

"But they kissed and everything."

"Still. They're being polite, but that's a long way from getting back together."

She pushed her lip out. "Dag." Then abruptly, "Michael's cute."

"Thanks. I like him."

"Do you guys kiss a lot?"

168

I clonked her over the head lightly with a present in a long box. "None of your business."

"You do, you do, I knew it." She cracked up in her most moronic way and then Aunt Hannah yelled for her to help carry something out of the kitchen.

We didn't, really. At first it was because I couldn't imagine kissing anyone but Misha, the cigarette way he'd smell and the imagined touch of his hands. Kissing isn't the biggest part of what I like about Michael. I like talking to him, sitting in Central Park watching the light change with him; his face when we were at the ballet. I didn't feel ready for tons of kissing and all that stuff. And he wasn't pushing it on me.

I went back to the sofa and was sitting with my dad and Stacey and Debbie just making party chit-chat. When I was little and my parents had parties, I would watch people sitting and talking like this, everyone holding drinks, and think there was nothing duller in the world. But now I can do it. I don't always find it riveting but I can do it, which is weird. I never thought I'd ever be able to sit around and talk. Just like I never thought I'd be able to do a triple pirouette. But now I can do both things. After a while, my mom and Hannah came out of the kitchen and said in fake British accents, "Dinnah is served."

We all went in and ate. The chicken was perfect and everybody told Aunt Hannah so a million times. I even broke down and had one extra piece. You should have seen the look Stacey gave me. "It's my birthday. I can go a little crazy," I said when I caught her eye.

"I think it's great. I've just never seen you eat so much at once before."

"Well, I'll go back to the usual diet tomorrow."

Everyone was talking and laughing at once. My parents had carefully chosen seats at opposite ends of the table so they didn't have to talk at all. But they weren't fighting or obviously avoiding each other. It was going okay. After we all ate, Hannah came out carrying this huge birthday cake with toe shoes made out of pink icing on it. They all sang "Happy Birthday" as loud as they could, with only Aunt Hannah on key. Then I cut up the cake and my mom took over passing it around and I just sat back and looked at everyone for a minute. I thought about the summer, the way I had felt about so many things when I got here and now, surrounded by everybody, how different I felt.

When my parents were first divorced, I thought I would have done anything to get them back together. But now, looking at my mom's face lit by the candles, I thought that she probably did the only thing she could do. Just like my dad. It still hurt, a lot, to see them apart. But just like with Misha, I had to stop kidding myself. They didn't belong together anymore. My life is separate from theirs and nothing will change that. My heart felt tight for a minute. When I looked at Stacey and Michael and Debbie, I felt like I could breathe again. Stacey was telling some long elaborate joke and they were all watching her, even Beth, waiting for the laughter they knew would come. *I can do that too*, I thought. I took a forkful of cake and waited.

Chapter Fifteen

"I had a great time at your house for your birthday," Stacey said. "Your parents are really cool. It's too bad they couldn't hang."

"Yeah, well, it happens to the best of them."

"You got that right." We were talking and stretching in the studio on the last day of class. The studio smelled like it always did, like rosin and sweat and the gluey scent of the rubber floor. Stacey was leaning on my legs, then I'd lean on hers, just like we had all summer. Except this was the last time we were going to do it. My throat closed up just thinking about it. Stacey seemed to be feeling the same way. She didn't talk nearly as much as usual. After a long silence, though, she said, "You wanna come by my room after class to wait for them to post the notice?"

I said yes. This was the day that we'd find out who got invited back for the fall and who didn't. My stomach pulled a little bit every time I thought about it. It was almost worse than waiting to hear if I'd been accepted for the summer.

There was something else too. I wanted to tell Stacey about Misha. She knew I'd been upset about something besides the affirmative-action thing, but when she'd ask me, I'd say it was nothing, that I was just worried about class or something. But now I felt bad that I hadn't told her. It would be a long time before I saw her again and she's one of my best friends now. She'd understand. But I was still nervous about telling her. What if she thought it was crazy?

We all got into place faster than usual when Miss Reinman walked in. While we were working on *tendus*, she came over and adjusted my foot briefly. I wondered if that was a good sign, if they thought I was worth working with enough to have me back. She moved on down the row without changing expression, just like usual. When we went to the floor for our combinations, she smiled a bit and said, "Let's go out with a bang. *Bourrée* into *grands jetés*, everyone." Miss Kaplan, the pianist, started playing the music from *Don Quixote*. Usually she just played things like "Oklahoma" or "Beer Barrel Polka" but for the last class, I guess she wanted us to feel like real ballerinas so she played all real ballet music. I loved it. My heart was pounding as we took turns across the floor. When I made my little runs on pointe and leapt into the air for the *jeté*, it was like I was flying. I could feel that it was right. My legs still hummed when the combination ended.

The music stopped and class ended with the usual bows a few minutes later. At the end of class, before we all lined up to thank her like we always did, she even said, "Girls, I know not all of you will be asked back for this fall. I just want to let you know that it's been a pleasure teaching all of you and that it's your love of the dance that's the important thing—whatever you go on to become." We applauded extra long after class. When I got up to her in the long line to murmur "Thank you, Miss Reinman," I tried to put a little extra emphasis into my words. I really did feel like she cared about all of us and that she liked teaching. I would miss her. She was shaking everybody's hand because it was the last class; she seemed to hold mine for a second longer as I thanked her. "It was a pleasure to work with you, Miss Harris," she said, smiling. I couldn't say any more, only smile my biggest smile back at her.

$\mathcal{W}$e changed quickly and walked through the bright end-of-summer day to Stacey's dorm room. The plaza was covered with people unwrapping sandwiches and holding their faces up to the sun. All the actors sat in a little knot at the reflecting pool near Juilliard, flipping their hair and gesturing dramatically. They stood out as much as us dancers with our pulled-back hair and turned-out duck walks. As soon as we got to Stacey's room, she threw her dance bag down on the bed and flopped down beside it on her back. "Off my feet at last. Do you ever feel like your feet are just going to fall right off?" she asked, flipping over to her stomach.

I laughed. "Yeah, sometimes."

We were quiet for a minute, then Stacey spoke. "So, Vick. What's up? Sometimes I feel like I'm saying that to you all the time," she said, wrinkling her nose. "But you never cough anything up on your own."

She was right. I sighed. "I know. And you're my best bud. And I haven't told you about this thing." I didn't know what to say. I decided just plunging in would be the best way. "I'm . . . well, I *was* madly in love with Baryshnikov, you know? You've seen my room and everything, right?"

175

"Yeah, sure. I get it. You know how I am about Keanu Reeves."

"Well, I went to see him—Baryshnikov, I mean—at Macy's that day when I missed class a week ago. I don't know; it was stupid. I thought he'd see I was extra good or something." I took a deep breath. "Anyway, it was a disaster and now I feel stupid for even thinking about him. He's a million years old anyway." I hid my face in my hands.

Stacey was quiet for a few minutes. Then she said, "I don't think it was stupid to go see him. I think it's cool that you wanted to see what would happen. So what are you going to do now?"

"Nothing. The summer's over. He's not going to come riding in on his white horse and sweep me off, that's for sure."

"Nope." She paused. "Do you think you're going to get asked back for the fall term here?"

This would be the first time I said it out loud, but somehow, having talked about Misha made it easier. Everything was in the open. "No, no I don't. Do you think you will?"

"Nope. That's okay, though. I miss Chicago. And I'll tell you something. I'm not even sure I want to keep doing this. It's getting harder and harder to keep grinding away in these classes. Maybe I should just do modern or something."

"I don't know. I still want to do it. I just don't think they're going to invite me back this fall. I'll have to push really hard at home this year and try for next year."

"Yeah, whatever," said Stacey. "You got the fever, girlfriend. I hope it stays with you. I feel like mine's burning out."

After a minute, I went and sat next to her on the bed and gave her a long, awkward hug. She hugged me back, then grabbed my hand. "Birth to earth?"

I grabbed her hand back. "Womb to tomb." We got that from that eternal friendship thing Riff says to Tony in *West Side Story*. We've both rented it about fifty million times. I took a deep breath. "Seriously, Stace, thanks for everything. I'm going to miss you."

"Yeah. You too, Mrs. Baryshnikov."

I grabbed a pillow from behind me and hit her in the head with it. She deserved it. Then we both fell over laughing.

There was a knock on the door and Stacey yelled, "Come in!"

Debbie came in and flopped in Stacey's desk chair. "I'm gonna faint. I can't wait until they put that stupid notice up and this is over," she said loudly.

"Oh, girl, you know your butt's gonna get asked back," said Stacey.

Debbie drew herself up very straight. "I don't know any such thing. I hope so, sure, but I don't know so."

Stacey and I just exchanged a look. It was normal to be nervous, but she really didn't have a lot to be nervous about.

Debbie looked at the clock and suddenly shrieked. "It's ten of. Let's get over there!"

A lot of people were already by the bulletin board by the time we got there. Stacey and Debbie and I stood close to each other, looking hard at the long list. No Rogers. That meant Stacey hadn't been asked back. And no Harris. That meant I hadn't been asked back either. Even though I had thought that's what would happen, I felt my heart squeeze in my chest. I'd thought maybe, just maybe. Then my eye fell a little lower, to Turner. There was Debbie's name. She saw it at the same time Stacey and I did. We all stood stock-still for a moment, not even breathing. Then we all started screaming at once. "Oh, Deb, you're so lucky. I can't believe it!" Stacey yelled. Then she hugged her, then I hugged her, then we just stood there looking at her name like it was going to vanish off the paper or something. All the other girls who had gotten in were doing pretty much the same thing, but most of the others who hadn't had slunk off, their heads lowered, some crying.

I always thought that I would be one of those who cried if I didn't get to stay here in the fall. I used to think that I would just die, that I'd jump off a building or something, but now that it had happened, I realized I honestly didn't feel like crying. I was sad, disappointed, yeah, but I didn't feel quite as awful as I'd always imagined I would if this moment ever came. I remembered the way I'd felt doing that final *jeté*. Like I could fly; like I could do anything. I could hang on to that feeling no matter what. I didn't need SAB for it, I didn't need Misha for it. I didn't have anything to prove. Knowing that isn't a bad way to end up. I hugged Debbie once more and then Stacey just because. Then without a word, the three of us ran to the door and burst out of it into the sunlight, laughing. I could still hear music in my head.